ANNIE'S ATTIC MYSTERIES ®

A Spicy Secret

D. Savannah George

Annie's™
AnniesMysteries.com

Library of Congress-in-Publication Data
A Spicy Secret / by D. Savannah George
p. cm.
I. Title
                    2012915726

AnniesMysteries.com
800-282-6643
Annie's Attic Mysteries
Series Editors: Ken and Janice Tate

10 11 12 13 14 | Printed in China | 9 8 7 6 5 4 3 2 1

―Dedication―

To the little girl I used to be, who wrote and illustrated her own stories, and to all the little girls who dream of one day being a published author: Never give up and your dreams can come true.

"You will never guess what we found yesterday!" Alice MacFarlane exclaimed, limping into A Stitch in Time for the regular Tuesday meeting of the Hook and Needle Club, the first after New Year's. She carried a covered glass dish, while a bulging plastic bag hung off one arm. Her project bag was slung over the other shoulder.

The ladies who had already arrived for the meeting were on the edge of their seats—the scent wafting from the dish was far more tantalizing than Alice's announcement, providing a nice distraction from January's low cloud cover and blowing snow.

Annie Dawson, close behind Alice, set down some bags and shrugged out of her winter wear—a white puffy down coat, gloves, hat, and scarf. She hadn't put much thought into her attire that day—she was just too excited about their discovery. She had barely run a comb through her blond hair, and she wore an old pair of khakis and a white sweatshirt that read "World's Greatest Grandma" in colorful puffy fabric paint, a handmade Christmas gift from her twin grandchildren, Joanna and John, now almost eight years old. She appreciated the sentiment, but under normal circumstances would have never worn it out in public. What if a certain mayor—Ian Butler by name—saw her dressed like this? Yes, she *was* a grandma, but she didn't need to dress like one. She vowed to go straight home and change after the meeting.

Annie relieved Alice of her burdens, placing the dish and bags on a little table that Mary Beth Brock, the shop's owner, had hurriedly set at the side of the room near the cash register. Mary Beth was also dressed for the cold, but she wore brown leggings instead of slacks, topped by a cream wrap sweater, making her look younger than her sixty years.

Peggy Carson, her short dark hair pulled back in blue kiddie barrettes, jumped up to help. Her pale blue turtle-neck and blue corduroy pants nicely set off her dark brown cable-knit sweater. Annie liked seeing Peggy in something other than her pink-and-white waitress uniform from The Cup & Saucer, but she knew the younger woman usually came to meetings during a break before the lunch rush.

"Peggy! You're not in your uniform! Are you not working today?" Annie asked her.

"Emily has a dentist appointment at one o'clock, so Jeff told me to go ahead and take the whole day off," Peggy told her as the two busied themselves with the paper plates, napkins, and plasticware. Annie found it amusing that the younger woman couldn't stop herself from serving, regard-less of the situation.

Alice—whose auburn hair looked perfect despite the weather—took off her long leopard-print coat and match-ing gloves, revealing a plum-color turtleneck sweater, lots of long, shiny necklaces, and a pair of faded jeans. She hung her coat on the rack in the corner before collapsing dramati-cally into a chair and putting her left foot on a stack of boxes.

"Sprained ankles are not for the faint of heart," she

announced grandly. "I will surely be glad when this winter is over." Alice had slipped on ice and had twisted her ankle over the weekend.

"I'll be glad too, and we've got months to go," said Kate Stevens while emptying and pricing a box of new yarn and pattern books. "This weather is just depressing." Kate wore one of her own crocheted creations, a long red sweater-vest, over a black top and black pants. Annie marveled, not for the first time, at how much talent Kate possessed and how lucky Mary Beth was to have her working in the store.

"You're telling me," Alice replied. "If I don't see another snowflake or ice patch for the rest of my life, it will be too soon."

"Enough chitchat," teased Mary Beth. "What did you find?"

"You know how I've been working on renovating Grey Gables?" Annie said, to everyone's affirmative answer. "Alice has decided to buy the carriage house, and she convinced me to help her start updating it. And, well, you'll never guess what we found!"

"That's wonderful, but I think I'm more interested in what's in this dish," Peggy laughed, lifting the lid and taking an appreciative sniff. "It smells divine. What is it?"

"It's an experiment," Alice replied, waving her hands grandly. "I guess I'd call it bread pudding since it's got bread, milk, margarine, eggs, and raisins in it."

Peggy grabbed a serving spoon from one of the bags and started dishing out the contents, taking a plate to each lady in the circle.

Stella Brickson, the matriarch of the group, took the

proffered plate with a murmured "Thanks." Whatever the situation, Stella always dressed impeccably; today she wore gray creased slacks and a black sweater adorned with a vintage art deco pin, her camel-hair coat draped casually over the back of her chair.

"Thank you, Peggy," Gwendolyn Palmer said, dressed in brown tweed like she'd just come from a photo shoot for a magazine.

Once everyone had a plate, Alice announced cheerily, "*Bon appetit!* Dig in."

The ladies each put a heaping spoonful in their mouths, only to make faces of disgust and spit it out immediately. Except for Stella, of course—the older lady's refined manners, even when confronted with such a vile taste, required her to discretely remove the offending substance from her mouth with one of the paper napkins Peggy had given her.

"Oh my, Alice, what in the world is this?" Kate was the first to ask what everyone else wondered. "And why does it taste so bad?"

"I'm not sure," Alice said, a mortified look on her face. "I was so short on time that I didn't try it. I just made it, and I wanted to share the experiment with everyone. My baking has never backfired like this before!" Alice then explained the discovery that she and Annie had made the previous day.

*   *   *   *

"Annie, Annie, Annie!" Alice whined into the receiver as soon as her friend answered. "I'm bored. I'm bored and cold, and my ankle hurts, and there's nothing to watch on TV. Will you come over? Pretty please?"

Alice did not feel like her usual indomitable self; instead, today she felt like a churlish teenager. The lovely Maine winter with its picture-perfect snowfall had disappeared a few days before Christmas in a terrible nor'easter, and the lights and excitement of Christmas had gone. Then, during Stony Point's New Year's Eve celebration two days earlier, she had slipped on a patch of ice and sprained her ankle.

Even the thought of buying the carriage house and making it her own, after all the years of renting, couldn't cheer her up. The carriage house—a miniature version of Grey Gables—had been part of the estate owned by Elizabeth and Charles Holden, Annie's grandparents. Betsy had sold it and the corner lot it stood upon several years after Charles's death. But now the furnace needed to be replaced—and badly. Repair work the owners had had done on it the previous month had been a Band-Aid fix at best.

But no matter how bored or cold or cooped up she felt, she would *not* walk to Grey Gables in the cold and snow on that hurt ankle, especially after the doctor had expressly forbidden such shenanigans. But she still felt a little silly, begging like that.

"No problem, Alice," Annie answered promptly. "I just took a chicken potpie out of the oven. Shall I bring it over?"

"Pretty please?" Alice asked, and Annie just laughed.

"I'll be right over," she said as she hung up.

Alice sighed and looked around. After she and John MacFarlane had divorced, the carriage house had been a cozy haven, and the years living next door to Betsy had made the time fly by. That was before Betsy's death and Annie's return to Grey Gables and Stony Point, Maine, a move that allowed Annie and Alice to rebuild a friendship begun in the summers of their youth, when Annie stayed with her grandparents while her parents served in overseas missions.

Alice loved her home's charm—the high-ceilinged foyer with its pretty chandelier and marble floor, the lovely windows, and the view of the sea from the porch. And its size was perfect for her lifestyle. But she felt dissatisfied with the wall color and the floor coverings, not to mention the furniture, much of which the current owners, the Swanns, had left from their days of using it every summer. To make matters worse, the day after Christmas she'd decided to empty the storage unit she'd rented after her divorce and go through everything—which meant she was now surrounded by boxes and boxes of items from her former life.

Although she'd gotten permission from the Swanns to begin renovations, and felt anxious to start, the mess, her hurt ankle, and a blue mood didn't make it easy. Hopefully, Annie would have some ideas.

"Come in," she hollered when her friend knocked. "I'm in the living room."

She waited impatiently while Annie fussed in the kitchen, setting the potpie to cool on a trivet.

"My stars, Alice! What in the world has happened?" Annie said in disbelief as she looked around the messy living room—boxes scattered all over the floor; blankets and bed linens piled on an end table; and the coffee table stacked high with mail, magazines, books, and catalogs. Even the bookshelf, normally a neat display of Alice's cross-stitch pattern books, a few treasured storybooks from her childhood, and a small collection of knickknacks, had been stuffed to overflowing. "I've never seen this place in such disarray! Are you OK? And are you warm enough under all that?"

Alice was huddled on the couch under a blue cotton blanket, a colorful block quilt, a black-and-white fleece throw, and a pink crocheted afghan, and she wore some sweats that had been through the washer so many times they barely had any color left. Her ankle had been wrapped in a brace, and she had it propped up on a heap of pillows.

"I'm warm enough—thanks for asking! And all this?" Alice dramatically swept her left arm to encompass her surroundings. "Since I'm officially moving on with my life by purchasing this place, I decided I should go through all the stuff I had in storage and put it behind me once and for all. So I emptied out the storage unit and brought everything here. Kind of depressing, actually, to look at things that used to belong to John and me, the couple. Then I twisted my ankle, so I'm feeling even more out of sorts. Unfortunately, what you see here isn't even all of it; there's more upstairs."

"Oh, Alice, you poor thing." Annie made her way carefully to her friend and then leaned down and gave her a hug. "How can I help?"

"Well, first, you can help me sort through and haul off the things I don't want to keep. And since the Swanns have said I could, I'd love to start renovations. But where should I start? Fresh paint on the walls? New rugs? New furniture? Throw everything out on the lawn and start completely over?"

"I don't think it's quite *that* bad." Annie laughed. "And of course, I'll be more than happy to help you go through the boxes. As for renovations, there are plenty of easy things we can do. After painting so much of my house, I can certainly help you pick colors. What if you have Wally redo the floors, and then decide what to do next? You know, start at the bottom and work your way up?"

Wally Carson, Peggy's husband, had been a godsend. There seemed to be no end to his knowledge of construction and renovation, and Annie knew that his work on Grey Gables's endless repairs really helped keep the Carson family afloat.

"Ooh, that's a great idea," Alice said, struggling to sit up. "Oh dear, my leg has fallen asleep."

"That's what you get for being such a lazybones," Annie teased her, and then she started giggling, with Alice joining in. "I can tell you that Wally will want the floors cleared before he gets started, so let's see what we've got. You're lucky I'm wearing my work jeans and sweatshirt today. I vote we *don't* start in here."

With Annie's help, Alice struggled to her feet and limped along next to Annie while they surveyed the rooms.

Alice's kitchen appeared to be the one place untouched by the chaos in the rest of the house. It was clean and neat. "The kitchen is probably a bigger task than we want to worry about right now," Annie said. "You'll eventually have to decide what you want done. New cabinets or just paint the old ones? New appliances?"

"I've watched just enough renovation shows on TV to know only one thing—it's almost too overwhelming to know where to start," Alice replied. "I know I don't like the flooring in here, but beyond that ...."

"OK, so we'll worry about it later." Annie stepped into a tiny, clear corner of the dining room, stacked with boxes and supplies for Divine Décor and Princessa, the businesses Alice worked for. "Wow! I do not want to try to move all those!"

"I know," Alice replied with a grimace. "Normally everything's upstairs in the spare room, but I had to move the boxes down here so I'd have space for sorting. And that's more than I usually have on hand; I just placed a big order from the end-of-year sales. I like to start getting ready now for spring parties."

They climbed the stairs to the second floor.

"I don't think we should try to tackle your bedroom until you've had a chance to sort through," Annie said, peeking in at the clothes, jewelry, shoes, magazines, books and half-finished needlework projects. Lotions and potions were scattered and piled on every available surface, including the bed. Annie was surprised at the mess; Alice was usually so together.

"I know," Alice groaned. "First I brought the storage unit stuff in here and started sorting, and then I thought I should use the excuse to go through my closets and drawers and everything else. Then I slipped and hurt my ankle. I just got overwhelmed and gave up. Why do you think I'm sleeping on the couch?"

"What about starting with the sitting area?"

"Nah, it's too small to make me feel like we've made a difference," Alice replied. "Why don't we start with the spare room?"

Annie took a look. "I think we have a winner!"

Alice went into her bedroom and turned on the radio. With Alice directing, and both of them singing along to the music, Annie moved everything in the closet to the sitting area, slid an empty chest into the hallway, carted a small table downstairs to the dining room, and dismantled and moved the twin bed into the sitting area.

"I must love you a *lot*," Annie teased as she wiped a hand across her sweaty forehead.

"Indeed, you do," her friend teased back. "And I certainly have never helped you move *anything* at Grey Gables, have I?"

"Not that I can recall right now," Annie retorted playfully, remembering the dozens of times Alice had helped her move boxes, chests, and myriad other things to or from the attic at Grey Gables. "Now, with all that out of the way, we can move this rug and see what's under there. But you've got to help me. I am *not* going to roll it up by myself." She surveyed the near-empty room and then added dryly, "Despite your life-threatening injury, I'm fairly certain you can sit on the floor and help."

"Fine, I'll help," Alice mock-grumbled, gingerly getting down and grabbing the end of the floral monstrosity. "One, two, three," she chanted, and they both started rolling, perfectly in time as if they'd been rolling rugs together all their lives.

Dust rose as they inched along, making them both cough.

"Well, what are you waiting for?" Alice asked when Annie stopped inexplicably, mere feet from the end.

"I have no idea. The rug is stuck on something."

Annie wiped her hands on her jeans and then ran one hand under the rolled edge.

"Just what I figured; some threads are caught. Hang on a second and don't let this thing go," she directed. "I can just see the headline in *The Point*: 'Local woman flattened by runaway rug; best friend to blame for her demise.'"

"Forget *flattened*. You're lucky I'm holding this side, or you would get *smacked*," Alice said.

Annie ignored her and carefully lifted each tiny thread from a floorboard. "OK, I'm done."

The two finished the task, and with Annie doing most of the heavy lifting, leaned the rug against the wall.

"Hey, Annie, look at that board," Alice said from her spot on the floor, pointing at a piece of a plank about eighteen inches in length. "It's a completely different finish, and doesn't even look like the same kind of lumber."

Annie examined the plank of the old wooden floor. "It looks like Grandpa or someone had to do some repair work on the floor," Annie said. "Doesn't look like they did a very good job of it, either. See? This part of the plank wasn't nailed in as securely as the original boards. It warped a bit, and now it's loose."

Annie kneeled down to run her fingers along the side of the board; Alice scooted over next to her, doing the same. Annie put pressure on the opposite end of the plank, and the slight warp helped pop the board out with just a little tugging.

"Look at that!" Alice exclaimed when the light revealed a small hidey-hole beneath the board. The friends began pulling out the contents—a faded brown fabric square wrapped around a spatula, a dull knife, a small bottle with an ornate label that said "The Spice Café," and a dusty old mason jar, the ring and lid long since rusted together. Once they cleaned off the jar, they could easily see the contents—small sheets of paper, most with handwriting on them.

"Try to get it open," Annie implored as Alice wrestled with it.

"I'm trying, but it's stuck."

Annie and Alice decided to take their newly found treasures to the kitchen, where they worked to open the jar. After several attempts—banging the jar upside down and running hot water over the ring—it loosened enough that they could remove it. Finally, they used a knife to pry up the lid a tiny bit until it gave way so unexpectedly that the jar's contents flew all over the floor.

"Well, this certainly *is* odd," Alice said, attempting to collect the sheets into a tidy pile. "Looks like this jar is full of recipes. But they are pretty smudged, and there are lots of question marks and other odd squiggles."

"Why would anyone hide a jar full of recipes under a floorboard?" Annie asked, wiping her forehead and squinting at a recipe that appeared to have been written in the dark.

"Well, Annie, m' dear," Alice said, "in addition to a nice cleared floor for Wally to work on, it looks like we've got ourselves another mystery!"

*   *   *   *

After Alice and Annie shared the story of their discovery, Peggy, excited as usual at the prospect of a mystery, asked, "Why would someone hide recipes in the floor? It's not money or jewels or a treasure map or a dead body."

The ladies laughed, and Alice said, "I for one am glad it's not a dead body. But it's just recipes, for heaven's sake, and in the carriage house! Why would anyone feel the need to hide them?"

"And more importantly, who would do that?" asked Stella, brushing imaginary lint off her slacks. "I would assume someone who lived in the carriage house would have done the hiding, but I certainly can't imagine why."

Kate stopped unpacking and pricing a shipment of buttons and leaned over one of the empty chairs. "That really is strange," she said.

"And why would anyone hide recipes that are so awful?" Mary Beth chimed in.

"Maybe I didn't get the recipe right," Alice said, "or maybe something is missing from the recipe. It was sort of hard to make out everything."

The ladies continued chatting, trying to come up with a reasonable explanation. After a few minutes, Gwen stood and discreetly gathered the others' plates still laden with Alice's "experiment" and took them into the back room to quietly empty them in the store's big trash can before settling back down with her knitting.

"That certainly is odd," Kate interjected, "but we have other important things to discuss. I know what our next group project could be." Her face glowed, just like it did every time she got excited about something. She picked up a stack of the latest edition of *The Point* and handed them out. "Clearly our esteemed editor, Mike Malone, had to dig to fill up even this one sheet, but look." She tapped the story on the front page, at the very top. "Some members of the Stony Point Community Church are going on a mission trip this June to Haiti. They plan to work in an orphanage and help build a school."

By now, Kate's face was so bright that she could have stood in for the light at Butler's Lighthouse.

"And how, pray tell, do we fit in?" asked Gwen, no-nonsense as always.

"We-e-e-e-ell ..." Kate drew the word out into four or five syllables, prompting Alice to throw a wadded-up napkin at her. "OK, I surrender! Our next project should be making blankets for the orphans. We can get the ladies at the senior center involved, and maybe the high school students too. I bet we could make a bunch of blankets by the time the volunteers go—maybe even one for each child."

As Kate talked, Annie smoothed her copy of *The Point* and read the short article, which included a map of Haiti and a photo of the church's pastor, to herself:

Reverend Roy Wallace from Stony Point Community Church will be leading a mission this June to Haiti, one of the poorest and least-developed countries in the world.

"I have been reading a lot about Haiti," Reverend Wallace said. "In recent years, the island has struggled with political upheaval, health crises, hurricanes, and that terrible earthquake. The children are the ones suffering the most—so many of them have been orphaned. Since children truly are our

future, we plan to visit an orphanage that currently houses about a hundred orphans and assist the organizers in any way we can."

Reverend Wallace said that the group also plans to help build a school at the orphanage.

"We hope the community will pitch in and help us with raising funds for building supplies and to help pay for our trip."

Annie felt overwhelmed with the thought of making one hundred blankets in less than six months, and she was also heartbroken that so many children had to live without parents. The story also made her think of her own missionary parents, who had spent so many years selflessly serving others.

"Don't forget the people working with the kids," Annie said suddenly. "I bet they could use blankets too."

"Indeed, they probably could," said Stella. "I say we find out if they do and get started right away—on the blankets *and* our new mystery."

— 2 —

The morning after the Hook and Needle Club meeting, Mary Beth and Kate sat at the table in the back room of A Stitch in Time, enjoying a cup of hot tea before they opened the store. Part office, part kitchen, part stockroom, and part break room, the space defied any and all attempts to keep it tidy. Even though business was slow, and they weren't ordering as much as they did during spring and summer, it seemed that wayward items ended up cluttering the space until both ladies wanted to scream.

"Seriously, how does this happen?" asked Mary Beth. "Thank goodness for my SUV. It feels like I take boxes to the recycling station every single day, and there's always more!"

"It's almost like they've told their cardboard friends that this is a good place to hang out," replied Kate. "And I swear I stock new items as soon as they come in, or store them on the shelves back here with the rest of our extra inventory, so where did this pile of embroidery thread come from? And it seems like pens usually walk off, so how did we end up with so many back here?"

"Beats me. We have to keep some boxes to pack up the blankets for the mission trip, and for when we have to ship something, but this many?"

Kate sighed and then brightened. "Speaking of the

mission trip," she said, "what do you think about using the store as a drop-off point for donations? That way, there would always be a place during business hours for people to bring the blankets they've made."

"That's a great idea. I knew I hired you for some reason other than your mad crochet skills!"

"Mad, huh? That means good, right?"

Mary Beth laughed. "It definitely means good. I think I've been hanging out with your daughter too much."

"Speaking of my lovely daughter, Vanessa mentioned last night that she has to do some sort of advertising project for her language arts class. I bet she and Mackenzie would be happy to make a flyer or something, if Mrs. Petersen lets them."

"That would be fabulous," Mary Beth said, looking at her watch. "Oops, opening time. Why don't you clean up back here a little while I open up."

"Gee, thanks. You are so good to me," Kate teased as the older woman washed out her mug and placed it in the drying rack next to the sink. She looked down at the trash can and groaned. "Ugh. The concoction Alice brought in yesterday is still in here. That's going out first thing."

Mary Beth started laughing. "I don't even think the stray cats will touch it."

Mary Beth went to the safe to get out the cash box before flipping on the light switches for the sales floor. In a few moments, Kate could hear the strains of music from the oldies station Mary Beth liked listening to.

Kate looked at her watch, and since school hadn't started yet, decided to call Vanessa. The school board hadn't been crazy about the idea, but had admitted—after parental pressure, of course—that cellphones at school could actually be good, at least from a safety standpoint. The kids had to leave their phones turned off during classes, of course, but were allowed to use them before and after school and at lunchtime.

Kate picked up her phone and chose Vanessa's name on her favorites list. There was just one ring before she heard her daughter's cheery voice.

"Hey, it's Vanessa. Well, my voicemail anyway. Close enough. You know what to do if you want me to call you back. If you don't, oh well. Have a super lovely day."

"Vanessa, it's your mom," Kate said as soon as it beeped and before she could stop herself. She knew how ridiculous she sounded. Of course her daughter recognized her own mother's voice, but she still said it every time, so she continued: "OK, you knew that. Didn't you tell me that your language arts teacher wanted you to create some sort of advertising promotion? Well, we could use your help at the store. We're going to be making and collecting blankets for an orphanage in Haiti. Mary Beth and I thought you could make a flyer or something, if your teacher approves. Call me back when you get a chance."

She hung up, surveyed the room, and started tidying.

*   *   *   *

A little after noon, Kate joined Mary Beth in the front of the store to take a break and eat lunch. On slow days, they both liked to eat in the circle of comfy chairs near the

window, surrounded by all the beautiful yarns and threads
and paraphernalia needed to craft practically anything.

Kate handed Mary Beth the brown bag she'd shoved
into the fridge that morning and opened her own tote, a
mini cooler that looked like a paisley purse with "K" embroidered on the front.

"Thanks, dear," Mary Beth said. She put her knitting
on the chair next to her, opened the bag, and pulled out
yogurt and a spoon. She had decided to try to lose some
weight over the winter, and since it was too cold to exercise
outside, she figured she'd try eating healthier. "What haute
cuisine do you have today?"

"A ham sandwich, carrots, and chips," Kate replied.

Mary Beth finished her yogurt and pulled out a plastic
container of pasta salad. "This is better than what we had
for lunch yesterday," she said. "I hope Alice doesn't think
trying out more of those recipes she found will help solve
the mystery of where they came from."

"It *is* peculiar to hide recipes; it might be fun to figure out where they came from. I just really can't imagine
why someone would hide them, and believe me, I've tried to
think of a reason." Kate took a few bites of her sandwich.
"Get any customers this morning?"

"Just a couple, and only one bought something.
It's been so slow. I'm glad we don't have many days
like this." Mary Beth sighed. "At least it gave me some
time to start a blanket." She held up her knitting for
Kate to see.

"Oh, it's so pretty!" Kate exclaimed. "I especially like
how the gradients go from light pink to dark purple."

"I love it too. It's expensive yarn, but that's one perk of owning my own shop. I get it at cost!"

Kate started to reply, but her cellphone rang.

"It's Vanessa!" she said, punching the button to answer.

Mary Beth stole a couple of Kate's chips while the younger woman was distracted.

"Yes, the mission trip Reverend Wallace is leading." Kate paused and then said, "Uh-huh. You can have the original for your class, and we'll make copies." Kate paused again and took a bite of carrot as she listened to her daughter. "Of course Mackenzie can help." Kate contributed another "Uh-huh" and "OK" to the conversation before finally saying, "See you after school."

"I take it her teacher is OK with the idea?" Mary Beth asked as soon as Kate finished the call.

"More than OK. Vanessa said Mrs. Petersen is thrilled. Something about 'real-world application,' and 'happy to support,' and I'm not sure what else. That child can talk a mile a minute sometimes."

"I think she gets that from Mackenzie. After all, her best friend is a cheerleader," Mary Beth said. "Being peppy is in the job description."

"Yeah, but a teenager is hard enough to keep up with. I'd at least like to understand her. Thank heavens Vanessa isn't a cheerleader. Can you imagine me a cheerleader's mom?"

The two laughed at the thought, imagining Kate with big bows in her hair, wearing a "Cheer Mom" sweatshirt, and hollering things like "Throw that swagger!"

"All right. It's time for you to stop lollygagging," Mary Beth teased. "Quit being a diva and get back to work."

Kate laughed. She threw away the remnants of their lunches and continued with her tasks.

*   *   *   *

By four o'clock, the back room was as clean as it could be, considering. The trash had been carried to the dumpster, and Kate had sorted the wayward embroidery floss and put the skeins where they belonged in the display case. The vast array of pens—anything from plain ballpoint pens to a promotional pen from a dentist in Wiscasset to colorful felt-tips—had been tested on scraps of paper. The dry ones had been thrown away, while those that had passed the test were either put in the penholder next to the register or stashed in Mary Beth's desk.

She'd stacked excess inventory neatly on the shelves, opened and organized a pile of mail, color-coordinated the paper next to the copier, and broken down a bunch of boxes for Mary Beth to recycle. She'd even, in a burst of energy, scrubbed the tiny powder room, sink and microwave, and even their new refrigerator, although it really didn't need it.

"I'm worn out," Kate said, walking to the front and sinking down into the chair next to Mary Beth. "How's that knitting working for you? Do you feel tired and stressed out?"

Mary Beth laughed. "I don't know what your problem is. I feel quite rested and peaceful."

"I just bet you do."

"And I hear the back room looks awesome," Mary Beth added.

"It does indeed," Kate replied. "Did you make any more sales today?"

"A few. Mostly I've just knitted. I'm always so busy with the store, I don't get—or take—enough time for my own handiwork. I'd forgotten how peaceful it feels."

"Once I figure out the pattern, crocheting is definitely Zen-like," Kate said, stretching her arms over her head. "There's nothing like seeing yarn turn into something useful and beautiful."

The bell rang as Vanessa and Mackenzie rushed in from the cold, laughing about something that had happened at school.

"Hey Mom, hey Mary Beth," Vanessa said, putting her backpack in an empty chair.

Kate really wanted to grab a hug, but didn't want to embarrass her daughter. Vanessa was at the prickly age where one minute she'd snuggle with her mother, and the next she'd be embarrassed by Kate just saying hello. She took a non-prickly tack. "How was school today?"

The two girls started talking at once.

"Slow down, you two," said Mary Beth. "And one at a time. Your mom confessed to me today that she can't understand 'teen-speak.'"

"Ha ha, Miss Brock," Mackenzie said, sitting down and plopping her backpack on the floor. "Mrs. Stevens, if you don't understand us, how come you know so much about what we're doing?"

"Mother's intuition, I guess," Kate replied, smiling. Her daughter's friend was a genuinely kind person; she was one of those bright spirits that automatically cheers a person just by being in the same room.

"If that's what you want to call it, then OK," the girl replied with a smile. "So, what is it you want us to do?"

Kate explained about the group project and how they wanted to get the entire community involved.

"Since your teacher wants you to create an advertisement, we thought you could create a flyer that we'll use to let everyone know about the project and how they can help. I'll have to confirm with Reverend Wallace, but I think we'll need about a hundred and twenty blankets in order for every child and adult at the orphanage to get one."

The girls' eyes went wide.

"So this flyer is super important, huh?" asked Vanessa.

"Yes it is! Mary Beth has volunteered the store as a drop-off point. And we need lots of people to participate if we're going to make our goal," Kate replied.

"What if we make a poster to show how many blankets we've collected? Would you hang something like that in the store, Miss Brock?" Mackenzie asked.

"Absolutely! That's a great idea," Mary Beth said.

"May I make a blanket?" Vanessa asked her mother. "I've never crocheted anything so big, but I'd love to try."

"Me too!" said Mackenzie, who had been learning to cross-stitch. "I can't crochet or knit very well, but I'll give it a go."

Mary Beth looked up from her own knitting and smiled. "You girls are just precious. Go pick yourself out some yarn. My treat. Oh, and for the flyer, be sure to add that I'll give a 10 percent discount on yarn or other supplies for anyone who agrees to participate."

"Wow! Thanks!" the girls jumped up and ran to the yarn bins, talking excitedly and fingering the different types and colors of yarn.

"That's really generous of you," Kate said.

"Well, it's a great community project and all that," Mary Beth replied. "But I'm sure they'll make a fabulous flyer—which means we don't have to!"

By closing time, the girls had picked out some yarn—dark green for Vanessa, light blue for Mackenzie—had chosen an afghan pattern that used simple crochet stitches from a pattern book, and had done a few practice squares. They hugged Mary Beth as Kate shooed them out the door to go home.

* * * *

The next day, Mary Beth watched the store while Kate went to visit Reverend Wallace. Kate found him in the food pantry at the church, putting cans and other donations onto shelves. Even doing menial labor, he dressed nicely in a pair of pressed khakis and a long-sleeve polo shirt. Kate smoothed down her ankle-length paisley skirt, glad she had worn something nice. The minister was one of the kindest men she knew, but she always felt a little intimidated by his presence.

"Hello Kate! How nice to see you. What brings you here today?" he asked, climbing down from the stepladder.

"I'm here to talk about your mission trip to Haiti. The Hook and Needle Club would like to help."

"Wonderful! Let's step into my office where we'll be a little more comfortable."

He led the way to a small room near the back of the fellowship hall. Furnished in shabby but sturdy furniture, it had a view of the ocean from the windows in the left wall. A bookshelf filled the opposite wall. It was crammed with Bibles, Christian literature, dictionaries, thesauruses, concordances, and compilations of sermon notes, not to mention books on theology, prayer, evangelism, spirituality, and church history. Kate couldn't help but feel impressed by the vast number of books.

The minister indicated she should sit, and she did, finding the faded floral wingback chair quite comfortable. Reverend Wallace sat in his desk chair, putting his hands behind his head and leaning back, almost touching the large bulletin board on the wall behind him. It was covered with photos, inspirational sayings, church bulletins, postcards, and Bible verses.

"I don't think I've ever been in here before," she said, nervously plucking at her skirt. "That's quite a collection of books."

"It is, and believe it or not, I've read most of them. They come in handy when I'm writing my 'Wit and Wisdom' column for *The Point*, and for my sermons, of course."

"Do you have a favorite book?"

"That would be like asking me to choose my favorite parishioner." Reverend Wallace laughed, leaning forward. "But if pressed, I'd probably say my favorite is this Bible that June gave me as a wedding gift."

He picked it up from his desk and passed it to Kate, who carefully turned the gold-edged pages. The green leather cover was embossed with his name, and several pages featured beautiful full-color illustrations.

"I know it cost her more money than she probably had at the time, but it meant much more than that. I had truly chosen a helpmate. By giving me this Bible, she told me she supported me and my life's calling."

Kate closed it gently and handed it back.

"That's a sweet sentiment."

The minister agreed, touching the cover as he set it back down. "So, how can the Hook and Needle Club help us with our mission trip?"

"I read the article Mike put in *The Point*. For some reason, it really touched me. I can't personally go on the trip or donate much money, but I can crochet, and I have easy access to yarn. So I thought, why don't I make some blankets for them to take along to give to the orphans? And then I thought, why don't I get the club members involved? We always do a project, so I figured this would be a good one."

Reverend Wallace nodded as she continued.

"At Tuesday's meeting, I handed out copies of the newspaper, told them my idea, and everyone agreed we should make a blanket for each and every orphan. Annie Dawson suggested we make some for the people who work there as well. But before we get too far, I wanted to make sure it's a good idea, and that the orphanage can actually use blankets."

Kate had never seen the minister grin so widely.

"Oh, Kate, you have no idea how wonderful and generous that is! I corresponded with Father Bruno recently—he runs the orphanage—and he said they receive just enough monetary donations for basic necessities, like food and medicine, but don't have anything left over for other things."

"So, would a blanket be something good to give

them?" Kate asked. "Or would it be like giving an ice maker to an Eskimo?"

Kate grabbed a small notebook out of her purse and began scribbling down some details, knowing she wouldn't remember everything he told her. The ladies were sure to have questions.

"Father Bruno specifically mentioned blankets as a need. The island gets cool at night, but not cold, so they wouldn't need thick, heavy blankets. Also, many of the children in their care arrived literally with only the clothes on their backs. Yes, it would be a wonderful gesture. And if you sent one for each child, each of them could have something of their very own."

"What about the people working there? Could they use blankets?" Kate asked.

"Chances are they give whatever they have to the children, so I'm sure they could."

"How many people work in the orphanage?"

"I'll confirm with the Father, but I know there are about five people who work there on a permanent basis, and then at any given time they usually have fifteen to twenty temporary volunteers. Right now I have ten people from the church signed up to go with me, but that number may change."

Kate continued to scribble as the minister talked about Haiti, its needs, and the work the volunteers planned to do while on the trip.

"I'm especially excited about working with them on their school. They've got the structure mostly built, and it just needs finishing."

"I can't imagine how fulfilling it will be for you and everyone going on the trip."

"Yes—I'm sure it will be. In the meantime, I have a lot to do to get ready, including fundraising," Reverend Wallace responded. "Do you have any more questions?"

Kate told him that Mary Beth had volunteered the store as a drop-off point, and that Vanessa and Mackenzie planned to design flyers to request help from the community.

"Is there anything else they need to include in the flyer?" Kate asked.

The minister smiled. "No. I think you've covered everything. Checks can be made out to Stony Point Community Church and note 'Haiti' on the check. We will gladly take as many blankets as you give us. If I hear of anything else, I'll be sure to give you a call." Reverend Wallace stood. "Thank you so much for coming by, Kate. Your visit has truly been a blessing."

He escorted her to the door and waved as she got in her car. As she drove back to the store, Kate felt blessed for having visited him and for the knowledge that her little idea would make a big difference.

~ 3 ~

When Annie awoke that cloudy Friday morning, she discovered Boots, her lovable gray cat, curled into a ball on her left side. Loath to get out of the warm bed, she sat up against the pillows, pulling on the pile of blankets and quilts until it once more tucked under her chin.

"Boots, I sure am glad you're here," said Annie to the cat, who by now was licking her paws and blinking. "With you here, I'm not just talking to myself."

Annie loved Grey Gables, but like most old houses, it was drafty and cold in the winter. Days like this made her miss her late husband, Wayne, even more than usual. On the few cold days they'd have in Texas, he would make her hot cocoa and bring it to her in bed. He also had an uncanny ability to find where drafts were coming in. His efforts always seemed to instantly make her feel warmer.

Despite its chill, Annie felt thankful for the old house, the blankets piled on her, and the quilts that had been handmade with bits of old cloth. She could almost hear Gram's voice saying "Waste not, want not," as she had many times during the summers Annie had spent with her. She looked around the room, grateful for Gram's loving care of everything.

But she also felt a tinge of guilt for all of her blessings, when there were so many needy kids.

"Well, Boots, thank heavens for all that yarn I have

on hand." She threw off the covers, eliciting a disgruntled meow and an injured look from her feline companion. "Oh hush, cat. If I get up, then you'll get breakfast!"

Annie threw on her usual wintertime work clothes—a pair of jeans and a sweatshirt. A trip to the attic was in order to retrieve yarn so she could start crocheting her first blanket for the group project. It seemed no matter how much time she spent in the attic—how much she discovered, and how much she cleaned—she always found something new, and she stirred up some dust. She also felt certain that Alice would call and request her assistance at the carriage house since she hadn't heard from her the previous day. The things they had found under the floorboard in the carriage house nagged at Annie, and she wanted to talk to her friend about it.

"I bet Alice will be bored again today. What do you think, Boots?" The cat just looked at her with a "like-I-care—feed-me" expression on her whiskered face. "Don't worry, little rascal. You'll get your breakfast!"

Before making a trip to the attic, Annie walked downstairs to the kitchen. She pretended to ignore the cat's clamor while she started a pot of coffee. She filled Boots's empty bowl with kibble before fixing herself a bowl of cold cereal and milk. When the coffee was ready, she retrieved her favorite mug and filled it, going to the window to enjoy the view of the ocean while she sipped her coffee. The clouds cleared, and the sun came out, cheering her immensely. Boots finished her breakfast, sniffed, put her tail in the air, and sauntered off to take a nap.

Her own breakfast finished, Annie washed, dried and

put away the dishes and then climbed the two sets of stairs to the attic. Opening the attic door, she was once again thankful that Wally had installed track lighting. The original lighting—a bare bulb with a pull cord—had been less than useful. And the small eyebrow windows on either side of the attic were more decorative than utilitarian. Not only did she have more light now, but she could actually point a lamp wherever she needed to be able to see.

She had stashed much of her extra yarn—a thoughtful and generous gift from her daughter, LeeAnn—in one of the many dressers Gram had stored in the attic. She and Alice had carried it down to the living room shortly after the treasure of yarn had arrived, only to lug it back to the attic after Annie discovered the dresser didn't fit with any of the decor in the room. She smiled and thought, *How could I ever say Alice didn't hoist her fair share of stuff around this house?*

She couldn't resist poking about in some of the boxes and bins surrounding the dresser. Even after doing so much to clean and organize, she still found something new on every visit. This short foray didn't yield much of interest: a bin full of old dish towels, another brimming with bank statements and cancelled checks from the 1950s, and a battered green hatbox stuffed with dribs and drabs of colorful embroidery thread. Annie once again heard an echo of Gram's voice saying "Waste not, want not," and smiled, imagining that many of those remnants were probably leftovers from a Betsy Holden Original, one of Gram's cross-stitch masterpieces for which she was revered. She set the hatbox aside in case Alice could use the contents in her own work.

Just one more box, and then I'll collect my yarn and get to work! Annie told herself.

She shifted yet another uninteresting bin and found a sturdy cardboard box, strapped in tape and labeled in Gram's strong handwriting: "From Charlie's desk."

As far as Annie knew, Gram had never emptied her husband's desk in the library—it certainly didn't appear to have been touched since he'd died, and she didn't think Gram would have ever gone through it when he was alive, either, just like Grandpa had never gotten into Gram's desk or cross-stitch supplies and projects.

Most of her grandfather's files and notebooks were on the bookshelf in the library. She had spent many a happy hour reading through the adventures chronicled in his meticulous journals. So what in the world could be in that box? And why would Gram have labeled it? Most of the things Betsy had stored over the years were not labeled and gave no indication as to where they had come from or why.

For some ridiculous reason, the box made her both nervous and curious. Annie grabbed it and carried it downstairs to the library and then went back up to retrieve the hatbox and a selection of blue and white yarns for her first afghan.

"Well, well, well," she said to Boots as she surveyed the labeled box, which she'd placed in the middle of the library floor. "I do hope this isn't yet another mystery to solve. I've got enough on my hands with those recipes we found in the carriage house."

With no food in the offing, Boots didn't reply, being far more interested in sunbathing on the window seat than worrying about yet another dusty old box.

"Fine help you are," Annie said, retrieving a pair of old office scissors from a desk drawer. In response, the cat rolled over, stretching her paws in the air to get some sun on her belly.

Annie knelt in front of the box. Inexplicably, her hand shook as she sliced through the tape. Whatever could Gram have packed away?

She lifted the flaps and almost laughed in relief. The box from the attic held patient files from her grandfather's veterinary practice. She suddenly remembered that he had used the carriage house as an office, and most likely had asked Gram to pack up his desk when he retired. She wondered if Cecil Lewey, who had assisted him on occasion, might have actually done the packing and then given it to her grandmother to store.

The phone rang, interrupting Annie before she could take anything out or really explore the contents.

"Hello," she answered, brushing some ubiquitous dust off her pants.

"Hi Annie!" Alice exclaimed.

"Let me guess. You're bored—right?" Annie teased.

"Yup. I sure am," said the voice at the other end of the line. "Not to mention my furnace decided to be difficult again today and it's freezing in here, so I can't do any sorting. Mind if I come over? I know I'm not really supposed to be walking, but I think I'll go mad if I stay here. And the sun has probably melted most of that evil ice."

Annie laughed at her friend's theatrics. "Sure, come on over. I want to talk about the recipes some more. Plus, you can help me look through a box I found in the attic."

"Sounds fun." Alice mock-groaned at the prospect. "See you shortly."

Annie went to the kitchen and put on another pot of coffee. She rummaged in her cabinets and found an open box of chocolate-covered shortbread cookies, arranged them on a plate, and put them on a small table in the library.

By the time Alice arrived, the coffee was ready. Annie settled her friend into the library's leather chair with a mug of coffee and pulled an ottoman over so Alice could elevate her ankle.

Annie sat in Gram's comfy chair, and the two sipped and munched companionably.

"OK—about the recipes. Things we know," said Alice.

"That should be a short list, but I'll get a pad of paper anyway," Annie said, retrieving a pen and notebook from Gram's desk.

"So," Alice said when Annie had sat back down, "one—we found the items in a hole under a floorboard in the upstairs spare bedroom of the carriage house. So they had to be placed there by someone who either lived in the carriage house or had easy access to it. It probably wasn't someone just passing through."

She waited while Annie scribbled before continuing. "Two—following the logic of the first item, the floorboard was a different wood than the rest. Someone had to have pried up the original floorboard, which would have taken some doing. It either got damaged or lost, so the person also had to find a plank to replace it."

"And no one noticed it all this time."

"Yeah, that's weird. So, three—that rug has probably been there for awhile."

"It was rather dusty," Annie noted.

"Four—we found a bunch of recipes in a mason jar, a square of fabric, a spatula, a knife, and a bottle labeled 'The Spice Café.' A rather pretty label, if I remember correctly."

"And the recipes were handwritten," Annie interjected.

"Handwritten, but mostly unreadable recipes," Alice agreed. "Except for the fabric, all of the items we found are used for cooking, so maybe the person who hid them worked in a kitchen."

"So what was the fabric for?" Annie asked.

"Who knows? Maybe just something to wrap around everything."

"So that's four things," said Annie. "What else?"

"Five—most of the recipes are handwritten, and some of them are unreadable."

Annie looked up from her notebook. "That's already in number four."

"Yeah, but I think it needs its own category," said Alice. "Since none of them were torn out of a magazine or newspaper, we can't date the recipes that way. Also, because some of them are scribbled and have strange symbols or notations, they may have been recipes in progress."

"Like when you sketch out a new cross-stitch pattern?"

"Exactly," said Alice. "They could be first or second drafts of a recipe. The ones that are readable could be final versions, or they could have been copied from somewhere else."

"So a cook probably hid the recipes."

"Probably. And that makes number six—someone who didn't cook would probably not bother."

"True. I know I wouldn't!" Annie said stoutly.

"Seven—the one recipe I attempted turned out awful."

"But what's the significance of that?"

"I'm not sure. But it must mean something," Alice said. "I think that's all we know."

"So, what do we do next?"

"I guess we can start asking around and find out what people know about the carriage house." Alice put down her coffee cup and clasped her hands together. "We always manage to solve these mysteries."

Annie laughed, put down her pen and notebook, and picked up her coffee mug. "Indeed we do, usually with a little help from our friends."

"Speaking of friends, I almost forgot I'm here on a mission of mercy. Whatever did you find in the attic this time?"

Annie pointed. "That box. It's labeled 'From Charlie's desk,' which surprised me a little. You know Gram never labeled anything. Oh, and this hatbox, which is full of bits of embroidery thread, probably left over from a Betsy Holden Original. I thought you might be able to use them. Somehow I doubt there's a big market on eBay for that sort of thing, even leftovers from a semi-famous cross-stitcher."

Alice laughed. "Probably not. Though I've heard about some weird things being sold, like a potato in the shape of Mickey Mouse, and some guy's leftover brussels sprouts."

"Eeew! That sounds disgusting," said Annie. "Maybe the thread would sell if it magically appeared in the shape of a rock star."

"Maybe. But let's not take the chance of that happening. I'll be a good friend and take it off your hands," Alice replied. "I know Betsy never could throw anything away, so some of it may be too short to do anything with. If I can't use it, maybe Mary Beth can use it at the store for her cross-stitch classes. Or perhaps I'll attempt that rock-star–shape thingy. Hmmm … Bruce Springsteen, maybe."

"Yeah, he's a good one. And thanks for taking these. Seems I inherited that 'can't-throw-anything-away' gene too."

"I do so appreciate that you've made me the recipient of your idiosyncrasies," Alice said, running her fingers through her auburn hair. "It doesn't look like you've gotten too far into that box yet."

"No, I had just opened it when you called. But it's clearly from Grandpa's vet days. I'm guessing it's from the desk he used in the carriage house. He probably made Gram label the box in case he needed it later."

"That's true," said Alice, "from what I remember. When I moved into the carriage house, Betsy told me some of the history. You remember that Captain Zacharias Grey built Grey Gables as a wedding present for his wife back in 1897, along with the carriage house. Back then, the first floor of the carriage house was the stable, and a little later, a garage. The second floor was living quarters for a servant or stableman. I moved in soon after my divorce, and you know how Betsy took me under her wing."

A sad, faraway look crossed Alice's face. "Your mom and Charlie were gone by then, and you were in Texas," she said. "I think both of us needed each other. I remember one day she was telling me about their early days in Grey

Gables." Alice shut her eyes and could almost hear Betsy's voice again.

*   *   *   *

"We moved into Grey Gables in 1947, the year after we got married, and just before I gave birth to Judy—Annie's mother. So much space for a baby and my needlework!

"The first floor of the carriage house—with a little bit of work—was the perfect place for Charlie's veterinary practice. He loved it out there. We liked to joke that our work areas—separate but nearby—were the key to our happy marriage. And when Judy got to be too much of a handful for one of us, we'd pass her off, one to another."

Betsy smiled as she thought of her precocious daughter and her dear husband—both gone now.

"Charlie didn't want to retire; he loved the animals and loved working with them. But we both knew it was time. He sold most of his equipment, and I packed up his desk, crammed with notes, patient files, and bills. For some reason, he wanted to keep those.

"After that, we turned the carriage house into complete living quarters, with the intention of using it as a guesthouse for visitors. We figured they would be more comfortable in their own space, and I wouldn't have to worry about having to clear a bedroom."

Betsy shared the scope of the renovation. They gutted the first floor and created a powder room, dining room, living room, and kitchen, along with the entrance foyer, and added windows to take advantage of the ocean views. In the upstairs—which already had a bedroom, bathroom, and small kitchen—they left the bedroom alone, but ripped out the kitchen, renovated the bathroom, and added a second bedroom, making it a compact two-story home. Like the careful edging on a wedding cake, they added a porch to match the one on Grey Gables, complete with gingerbread trim and white wicker furniture. They also planted rhododendrons and lilacs, most of which had survived the intervening years.

"After Charlie passed," Betsy said, a catch in her throat, "I just could not bear to keep the carriage house. Between the memories of him and the animals he treated there—plus just the upkeep on the place—I decided to sell it. We'd rarely used it as a guesthouse, so it just made sense to let it go."

After an exhaustive search for the perfect people to become her neighbors, Betsy sold the carriage house to a couple from New York, Yvonne and Arthur Swann.

"The Swanns are such nice people, and I really enjoyed having them as neighbors," Betsy said. "They used it as a summer home for many years, and would occasionally host parties for their 'summer friends,' as they called them. As they grew older, it was harder for them to make the trek up, so they decided to turn it into a rental property. Lucky for you and for me!"

*   *   *   *

Alice shook her head, bringing herself back to the present and taking another sip of her coffee.

"I think I was far more lucky than Betsy, to tell you the truth. I got to live next to her in a lovely place I could afford, and she gave me a kind and patient ear when I needed it."

"I wish I had come to visit her more," Annie said wistfully.

"She wanted to see you too, but she knew how busy life in Texas kept you," Alice replied. "She really enjoyed her trips to see you, I can tell you that. And she wouldn't shut up about how precious and cute and darling her great-grandchildren were."

"Well, they are at that! Who can blame her?" Annie answered, once again feeling slightly guilty for being so far away from her daughter and grandchildren. She resolved to have the whole family up to visit that summer, or else to go see them and spend a few weeks in Texas—maybe both.

"All right, quit being glum," Alice said, realizing that all the talk about Betsy had made Annie a bit melancholy. Annie was startled, forgetting that her friend could always sense her mood. "We've got a box to look through!" Alice put down her coffee cup and hobbled carefully to where the box sat. "Wonder if we'll find anything interesting?"

The two plopped down on the floor next to the box and emptied it in short order. Papers and files surrounded them.

"Boots!" Annie exclaimed as the cat settled on one of the stacks and stretched to her full length. "Why is it that cats have to be right next to you if there's paper or food involved?"

"The food part is easy," Alice laughed. "I'm not sure about paper or boxes. My sister had a cat when we were kids, and that thing just loved cardboard for some reason. I remember one time Mom had bought new dishes or something, and put the empty boxes in the mudroom. We didn't find that cat for two days because she'd curled up in one of them. Stuff had gotten stacked on top of it, and she couldn't get out. And she was one of those weird cats that didn't freak out if she got locked up somewhere."

"I'm pretty sure Boots knows better than to try something like that, living in the house where other people's belongings come to rest." Annie gave the feline a pat on her belly, and turned to the detritus around them. "I have no idea what to do with this after we go through it. I guess just box it back up."

The two friends stayed mostly silent as they perused the papers, interjecting on occasion if they found something entertaining.

"OK, these files are written neatly, but I think they're harder to understand than the recipes," Annie said. "Obviously, I get the animal's name and the owner's name, but what do you suppose 'imrab-1' means? Or 'dex sp'?"

"Beats me," said Alice. "All I know is that they are boring me to tears. Are you sure you even want to keep this stuff?"

"I have no idea. But you know me. It would be hard to just throw everything away. I guess I could ask Carla Calloway what she suggests."

"She is good with animals, but not so good with people," Alice replied. "There's no telling what she would say!"

Carla, a competent vet, ran a shelter for abandoned animals, but some people called her "Carla Callous" because of her brusque manner.

"That's a chance I'll have to take," Annie said. "Besides, she's been much nicer lately—to people, that is. She's always been nice to animals. I guess I could have Vanessa ask her. She seems to get along just fine with Carla."

"That's because Vanessa is an angel and puts up with her, but it's mostly because Vanessa loves the animals and likes volunteering at the shelter."

"I should also ask Cecil Lewey what he thinks. He may want to keep these, or at least look at them. Grandpa mentioned him quite a bit in his journals."

The ladies were quiet as they went through more of the files.

"Look at this ledger," Annie said an hour later. Most of the files were—as Alice had stated so eloquently—boring and had been put back in the box. The blue leather-bound ledger was a welcome find. "Sometimes Grandpa would settle a debt by accepting a tool or eggs or wheat or something like that in lieu of cash."

"That doesn't surprise me. Your grandpa never would let an animal suffer, regardless of the owner's financial state."

"And Gram didn't have to keep chickens to get fresh eggs for cooking! Seems I remember she liked chickens but didn't like their upkeep or them getting into her garden."

The ledger, written in her grandfather's neat hand, was a straightforward list with the date, animal name and type, owner's name, procedure, and the amount owed.

Annie missed her grandfather. She'd felt closer to her grandmother, probably because she'd helped Gram with chores—at Gram's insistence, of course—and the older woman had spent hours teaching her to crochet, while her grandfather had been busy with his practice.

She'd been a teenager when he'd retired. At that age,

she'd hung out with Alice and her other friends more than with her grandparents. But she had fond memories of rainy days or those days when everyone else was busy—she'd sit on the window seat of the library, working on a crochet project, while Grandpa sat at his desk and wrote in his journals, occasionally reading a short anecdote aloud. And she'd loved it when, as a child, he'd read her stories from *The Jungle Book* or other classics. She was nearly through with college when he died and was thankful for the years she had known him.

Annie decided to add the ledger to the bookshelf that held her grandfather's journals. Just holding it made her feel close to him.

"Looks like we're almost to the end," Alice said, nudging Boots off the last stack.

"Thank heavens," Annie replied. "I forget how tiring it can be to go through stuff."

They discarded the first few files without comment.

"Hmmm ... this one looks interesting," Alice said. "Apparently our esteemed mayor had a very sickly cat when he was a child." Annie tried to grab the file, but Alice kept it just out of reach. "Seems that little Ian liked to feed 'Banana' raw eggs, which caused the poor kitty's fur to fall out."

"Ian named his cat Banana?" Annie asked.

"Yes. And there's more! Seems after the raw eggs incident, our young friend decided that Banana needed some raw meat."

"And?"

"And that caused vomiting and diarrhea. For the cat, not Ian."

After a few minutes of laughing and playing keep-away,

Alice finally handed it to Annie so she could see for herself.

"I don't think I'll ever be able to look him in the face again," Annie said dryly.

"Me either. Or at least, not without giggling!"

At the very bottom of the stack sat a nice, slim container, in much better condition than the rest of the files.

"This looks rather official," Annie said, turning the box over in her hands and then opening it. "Look—here's a sticker that says 'Connor and Sheehan, Boston, Mass.'" Unfolding the papers, she let out a squeal. "Why, it's the building plans for the renovation of the carriage house!"

"Oh cool!" said Alice. "This is really neat." Together, they spread the blueprints out on the floor and examined the documents. "Here are a couple of sketches of what the interior and exterior used to look like."

"According to this, your spare room was the original bedroom," Annie said. "That means whoever hid the recipes could have lived there back in Captain Grey's era."

"Yeah, but it doesn't mean they weren't put there by someone who rented from the Swanns either."

"True enough, true enough," Annie said. She began folding everything up again. Once the pages were neatly placed back in the container, she handed it to her friend. "I think you should have these. After all, you're going to be the new owner of the carriage house and in charge of its history."

"Are you sure you trust me with this?"

"Absolutely! I'm also sure it's one less thing for me to worry about!"

*   *   *   *

After Alice had gone home, Annie fixed herself a light lunch and looked through some of Gram's crochet books. One of the books, with a copyright of 1979, instructed the crocheter to make forty-eight different squares in very dated shades of gold, light orange, and dark orange. Annie liked the patterns, but she decided that no one loved orange that much, and she knew that trying to figure out that many different stitches, along with the proper gauge, would take too much time.

She decided on two tried-and-true granny-square stitch patterns she'd made in the past and two different yarn colors—a pretty sky blue and white. Settling into the window seat with Boots and a skein of the blue yarn, she got started.

$$-4-$$

Kate didn't have to work at A Stitch in Time that Saturday, but she still got up at her usual early hour. She spent a lot of time working on a blanket for the project, and when her hands needed a rest, she looked out the kitchen window at the snow and thought about the recipes Alice and Annie had found. Of all the mysteries the club had encountered, this one seemed the silliest, and yet it was so intriguing. Try as she might, she couldn't remember anyone other than Alice living in the carriage house. And she couldn't imagine why someone would hide recipes.

She crocheted a little more, and then she flipped through one of her needlework books. She'd been collecting them for years, ever since Betsy Holden had given her a copy of *Crocheting for Beginners*. Betsy had patiently taught her first how to hold the hook, and then taught her all the basic crochet stitches. It wasn't long before Kate had mastered them and started crocheting more and more elaborate patterns.

Kate practiced crochet and spent as much time with Betsy as she could. Today she wouldn't give up her skill for anything in the world. She had been careful not to make her daughter feel like she had to crochet too, but Vanessa had happily taken up the crochet hook and learned basic stitches when she was merely five, and she had crocheted off and on as she'd gotten older. Mackenzie had only been introduced to needlework and crafting when she and Vanessa became friends, but she thought it was cool and always wanted Kate to make her things.

Kate smiled to herself. If a cheerleader liked needle-work, the other kids could hardly make fun of it. And *everyone* loved Mackenzie. So they might not love crochet or other needle crafts, but they would keep their opinions to themselves.

She glanced at the clock above the kitchen table. Mackenzie had come over to spend the night with Vanessa so they could work all day Saturday on the flyer about the blankets for the orphanage. It was already after ten o'clock; Mackenzie and Vanessa would eventually wake up and come out for breakfast. Kate had heard giggling when she'd woken up in the middle of the night to go to the bathroom, so it could be a while.

Kate had always loved to sleep in on the weekends, but her mother had never let her and had in fact been vehe-mently opposed to it. Kate had vowed back then to let her own children sleep as late as they wanted, as long as they got up on time for school during the week.

The phone rang, and she jumped up to grab it before it woke up the girls.

"Hello?"

"Hey Kate," she heard her ex-husband, Harry Stevens, say.

"Handsome Harry!" she heard herself reply, groan-ing inwardly. She hated that she still called him that after everything they'd been through. He was handsome on the outside, but *not* on the inside. Plus, calling him that only added to his oversized ego.

"Yeah, so I haven't had Scooter over for a while, and thought I should arrange for a weekend visit."

Kate smacked herself in the forehead. She and Harry supposedly had joint custody of Vanessa, but he rarely bothered to see his daughter. If he actually made plans, typically he'd back out at the last minute. To top it off, because they had joint custody, and he supposedly made less money than she did, he didn't have to pay any child support.

She wanted to scream at him, but replied calmly, "You know she hates that nickname." He'd christened his daughter with the name when she first learned how to walk—because mostly she'd scooted around on her bottom until she'd gotten the hang of standing up. Kate had found it cute at first, but at six years old, Vanessa had vehemently—and loudly—opposed the term, so she'd never called her that again. Harry, as usual, didn't care.

"Yeah, well, she'll always be Scooter to me. And what about it? When can I have her?"

That really set Kate's teeth on edge—Harry acted and spoke like Vanessa was another *thing*, rather than his only child. But she kept her tone and words as polite as possible, knowing that showing her anger would only make him more difficult to deal with.

"I'll have to check with her to find out her schedule. When did you want to get together with her? I know she's got projects due for school, and I seem to remember that one of her friends is planning a sleepover, but I'm not sure which weekend."

"Well, find out, would ya? I want to take her to the Maine Maritime Museum down at Bath. They've got a new exhibit on the scallop industry I'd like to show her."

She sighed as quietly as she could. "Harry, you know Vanessa won't want to go the Maritime Museum. Can't you take her to something in Portland that she'd actually *want* to do, like a Sea Dogs game or the planetarium?"

"Pshaw. Scooter likes seeing the boats. Besides, the Sea Dogs don't play in the winter. Duh!"

Her ex-husband, a third-generation Stony Point fisherman, owned and ran his own scallop boat and thought everyone was obsessed with the sea and everything to do with it. Vanessa had outgrown her fascination shortly after outgrowing her nickname, yet he refused to acknowledge it. Kate figured he still was mad that his only child had been a girl—he'd really wanted a son to work with him on the boat.

Kate clenched her fists in frustration. "All right. I'll ask her and get back with you."

"Cool. See ya," he said as he hung up.

She took some deep breaths to sooth her nerves and then went back to her book.

*   *   *   *

Later that afternoon, Kate sat in her favorite chair in the living room, crocheting on her first afghan for the Haiti project—using her very own pattern, of course—while Vanessa and Mackenzie sat on the floor, surrounded by art supplies of all kinds—paints, markers, pencils, poster board, stencils, and even a dictionary. The pair laughed as they came up with ideas for the flyer and the poster to track donations. They seemed especially tickled with the line "Heatin' Up Haiti," much to Kate's amusement, even though she had no idea why they found it so funny.

"Hey Mrs. Stevens, didn't Miss Brock say people could drop off their blankets at the store?" Mackenzie asked, putting aside a red marker and picking up a blue one.

"Duh," Vanessa teased. "*And* she said she'd give 10 percent off supplies. Weren't you listening?"

"Uh, yeah, but I still have a question for your mom."

Kate smiled. "Darling daughter, do try to be polite and let your friend ask her question."

"Whatev'," Vanessa said, tossing her hair out of her eyes. To anyone else, it might have seemed like backtalk, but Kate knew her daughter was just teasing.

"Anyways," Mackenzie said, "I wondered if Miss Brock might like it if we decorated a box for the store, where people could put their blankets when they're done. I bet our teacher would even give us extra credit for it."

"I'm sure Mary Beth wouldn't mind at all, but I'll ask her just to make sure."

"We just need a really big box to decorate," Mackenzie said. "Do you know where we can get one?"

Kate laughed. "Do I ever! We've got boxes up to our eyebrows at the store. I could run by and find one. And how about I pick up a pizza for dinner from Sal's Pizzeria while I'm out? I don't know how we survived before he opened."

"I do love his pizza," said Mackenzie. "I want pepperoni."

"I want veggie," said Vanessa.

"All right—you got it! Can I trust you two not to draw on the walls while I'm gone?"

"Mom!" Vanessa said. "We're not five years old anymore."

"I just never know with you two," she said, grabbing her coat and purse, and pulling on a pair of brown gloves and a purple hat. "I'll be back shortly, and woe unto you if the wall is damaged!"

"Mom! Seriously!" she heard as she went out the door to the garage. Then she heard Mackenzie's voice: "She didn't say a thing about the carpet."

*   *   *   *

Kate hated to leave the warmth of the house and face the gloomy, snowy day. But she also knew she could use a little time to herself, and a visit with Mary Beth would do her good. The girls had woken up not long after Harry had called, and she hadn't had time to really think about his request. She felt awfully irritated with the whole thing. In fact, practically every word that came out of his mouth irritated her. How dare he not take his daughter's feelings into consideration and act like Vanessa was a dog or a potted plant he could just pick up whenever he felt like it?

She hadn't yet mentioned the call to her daughter; she knew Vanessa would get upset and unsettled. The girl preferred not to think about her father. His violence had really affected her, and he continually reneged on promises. Kate knew she'd have to bring it up eventually, but for now she wanted her daughter to enjoy her day.

She arrived at A Stitch in Time a little after three thirty. Mary Beth sat in one of the comfy chairs, working on the blanket she'd begun earlier in the week.

"We're closed," the older woman said without looking up from her flashing needles.

"Sure you are," Kate said. "Your sign says you close at four o'clock, so you still must be open. And anyway, I planned to spend a whole bunch of money today. Guess I'll just have to go down to Finer Things and get rid of my cash there."

"Guess so," Mary Beth retorted, looking up. "I don't need your kind in my store anyway." They laughed as Kate sank down into the chair next to her.

"So, really, why are you here?" the older woman asked. "I'm pretty sure I gave you the day off, and it's practically time for me to get out of here."

"Ah, well." Kate heaved a sigh. "The girls are working on the flyer and asked if you'd be OK with them decorating a box to put in the store as a place to collect the blankets. I told them I'd ask and then pick up a pizza."

"And that makes you sigh, because?"

"*That* doesn't. Harry called this morning and wants a weekend with Vanessa, or 'Scooter' as he persists in calling her. And he gets under my skin like no one else. I still don't know why I ever married that man."

"Aw, honey, I'm so sorry." Mary Beth put her knitting down and gave Kate her full attention. She knew how much Vanessa hated that moniker, and she really hated to see Kate so upset. "You married him because you loved him, and you got a wonderful kid out of the bargain."

She leaned over and gave Kate a quick hug. "What does Vanessa say about it?"

"I haven't told her yet. He says he wants to take her to the Maritime Museum—as if she'd even want to do that, and as if he'd actually take her."

"He's not exactly one for keeping promises, is he?"

"No! I'm sick of having to clean up his messes, and I'm sick of him hurting our daughter. Plus, I don't know what weekend she's free. She's always so busy with school and her friends."

"Have you tried ignoring him?"

"Yes, but that ends up being worse." Kate sighed again. "He accuses me of keeping him from his daughter when I do that. Never mind that he's the one who stays away."

"I think all you can do is tell Vanessa as gently as possible, and then tell him when she's available and hope for the best."

"I guess you're right," she responded. "So, is it OK if the girls decorate a box for people to put their blankets in? Mackenzie said they might even get extra credit for it."

"Of course! Far be it from me to stand in the way of extra credit," Mary Beth said. "Would you like me to help you look for one?"

"Only if you can tear yourself away from that chair," Kate teased.

"Ha, ha. Thank goodness my assistant cleaned the back room," Mary Beth said. "Should be easy to find one that will work."

"I hear she's quite talented," Kate said.

"That's what I hear too," Mary Beth countered. "Hey!

How about the box the new refrigerator came in? We haven't gotten rid of it yet, have we?"

"That would be great!" Kate said. "I broke it down, but it would be easy to tape it back up. Plus the girls can cut it down to whatever height they need."

Mary Beth helped Kate load it in her car and then gave her a hug.

"Don't worry, Kate. Vanessa will be fine. You're a great mom. And soon enough she'll be eighteen, and you won't have to worry about Harry anymore. It will be up to her if she wants to see him or not."

Kate groaned. "Thanks, I think. I'm not sure I want to be reminded that my baby will be an adult soon."

"Well, she will be. We all get older, even if we don't grow up."

* * * *

Kate arrived back home, big cardboard box and two steaming pizzas in hand. She put the pizzas in the oven to stay warm and lugged the box into the living room. She smiled at the sight of two brown heads bent over a poster. It looked like a tornado had gone through the room and scattered art supplies to every corner. Thankfully, the walls were unmarked.

"Hey girls! Dinner's here, along with your box," she said.

"Hi Mom," said Vanessa.

"Oh hey, Mrs. Stevens," said Mackenzie. "Look! We're almost finished! What do you think?"

Kate walked over to the oasis of calm in the middle of

the floor. On the top of the poster and the flyer, they had written "Blanket Haiti" in big colorful letters.

"That's a great name for our project! Who came up with it?" she asked.

"I did!" Mackenzie piped up. "But it's not really my very own idea. My mom bought some sheets from a company called Blanket America. She told me they make a donation to the needy for each sale they make. I figured they wouldn't mind if I used that, since we're kinda doing the same thing, and they support Haiti too!"

"That's great," Kate replied, "and I love all the colors."

The flyer featured a tall stack of hand-drawn blankets, each one a different color—from bright blues and fluorescent pinks to pale greens and sunflower yellows.

Three poster boards taped together on the shorter ends made for a very tall tracking poster.

"Look, Mom. We drew the outline of forty blankets on this. You can color in a blanket for every three you collect!"

"How does this sound, Mrs. Stevens?" Mackenzie said and handed her the flyer.

Kate took it and read aloud:

Blanket Haiti.
Volunteers from Stony Point Community Church are heading to Haiti to be of service at Light of Hope Orphanage. In conjunction, the Hook and Needle Club hopes to make and collect at least 120 summer blankets for the orphans and the workers who care for them. Make one (or seven) or donate your like-new extras! They should be lightweight and twin-size. Drop off your blankets at A Stitch in Time before June

15. See Mary Beth or Kate at the store for more information. You can make a difference!

Kate turned to the girls. "Perfect! This is really wonderful. Mary Beth is going to be thrilled, and I'm sure your teacher is too. The only thing I see that needs changing is that you need to add that the church is accepting cash donations as well."

The girls beamed and went back to drawing.

"When do you want to eat dinner?" Kate asked.

"As soon as we're done with everything," Vanessa said. "Thanks, Mom!"

After dinner, Vanessa and Mackenzie covered the box in brown paper and wrote 'Blanket Haiti Blanket Drop' in large letters on one side and drew piles of multicolored blankets on the other three.

Mackenzie's mother arrived to pick her up a little before nine o'clock. The women chatted as the girls finished collecting the art supplies from various corners and even from under the couch, returning each item to where it belonged.

"Thanks, Mrs. Stevens, I had a lot of fun. And thanks for dinner," Mackenzie said, putting on her winter gear.

"You're very welcome," Kate said, giving her a hug. "You know you can come over and make a mess on my floor anytime you'd like. But the walls are still off limits."

"Mother!" Vanessa said, rolling her eyes in mock exasperation.

They said their goodbyes, and Kate and Vanessa collapsed onto the couch after Mackenzie and her mother had driven away.

"That was fun, huh?" Kate asked.

"Yeah, lots, but it was also tiring. I love Mackenzie, but she talks so much sometimes I just want to throttle her."

Kate leaned over and kissed the top of her daughter's head.

"I know what you mean," she segued. "Speaking of throttling, your father called this morning."

"Oh no! What does he want now?"

"He wants a weekend to take you to the Maritime Museum in Bath. I told him I'd find out when you're available."

"Mom, do I have to?" Vanessa's voice suddenly sounded tearful. "I don't want to go anywhere with him, much less to that museum. We've been there like a hundred times already. And all Dad wants to talk about is his boat."

"I know, honey, and I'm so sorry," Kate said, drawing her into a hug. For once, Vanessa didn't resist but curled up on her like she'd done as a little girl. "But he is your father, and you know how he gets if we try to ignore him. And I don't want to be dragged to court because he's mad."

She kissed the top of Vanessa's head. "And anyway, as a wise woman told me today, you'll be fine. And when you're eighteen you won't have to worry about it anymore. You can decide how often you want to see him, and you don't have to if you don't want to."

Vanessa smiled a little. "So, who was the wise woman?"

"Mary Beth, of course. I told her I didn't want to be reminded that my little girl is growing up."

"Thanks! I'll just have to remember that if and when Dad actually takes me somewhere."

"Good idea. Be sure to tell me when you have a free weekend, and I'll call him in the morning."

Kate yawned, and Vanessa followed suit soon after.

"Off to bed for both of us, I think," Kate said. "Sleep well, darling. I love you."

She was rewarded with a big hug and a whispered, "I love you too, Mom."

~5~

The morning of the next Hook and Needle Club meeting dawned bright and cold with a cloudless pale blue sky. Annie figured even the heavens were tired of being covered up.

The weekend had been positively dismal, with biting wind, blowing snow, and not a ray of sunshine. Annie and Alice had spent a lot of time together, sipping hot cocoa and watching DVDs of old movies at Grey Gables.

They had sung *You're the One that I Want* and had danced along to all the songs in *Grease*—though in Alice's case, she had mostly swayed back and forth to keep from re-injuring her recuperating ankle. Just thinking about it made Annie laugh.

"You look like a cross between Stevie Wonder and the Church Lady on *Saturday Night Live*," Annie had teased her friend.

"Well, that only proves how old you are," Alice retorted, doing a funky hip thrust. "These moves made me *very* popular in high school."

"I can only imagine," Annie replied dryly, getting a pillow in her face for her trouble.

They'd eaten way too much popcorn while watching *When Harry Met Sally* and had cried while watching *Steel Magnolias*. Somehow, they'd even managed to get some work done on their blankets for the orphanage. They had also spent time talking about the mystery of the recipes, but had made no real progress in figuring out why the recipes had been placed in the hidey-hole in the second floor of the carriage house. Annie had gotten out her notebook, but ended up adding nothing but doodles.

Annie woke up later than usual that Tuesday, and she had to rush around to get ready. Even in her hurry, she still felt positively cheerful. She dressed in a pair of dark jeans and a turtleneck, covering that with a green sweater. She pulled her hair—now in an awkward growing-out stage, courtesy of her last haircut—back into metal barrettes and put on a light coating of mascara and lipstick.

Satisfied with her looks, she went downstairs for a quick breakfast, fed Boots, and packed her tote bag with a skein each of her blue and white yarn, crochet hook, and the blanket she had started—so far she'd finished eighteen squares of the first pattern, nine in each color.

She was just putting on her coat when Alice called.

"Would you mind driving me to the meeting?" her friend asked. "I have such a load to carry, and my ankle is hurting again. It's so hard being me sometimes."

"It's hard being me sometimes too," said Annie in a teasing tone of voice, "especially when I have to listen to your whining."

"I'm not whining. I'm just stating a fact. The cold is making my ankle throb," Alice said in response. "So, would you pretty please drive me to the meeting? Plus, you know my Mustang does not look pretty in snow tires."

"And my car does?" Annie retorted. "Plus, in case you haven't noticed, your Mustang *does* have snow tires on it."

"Yeah, yeah. OK, you got me. Can I have a ride anyway?"

"No problem—as long as you don't make me later than I already am!"

They hung up, and Annie finished buttoning her coat. She pulled on her fleece-lined gloves and wound a thick brown scarf around her neck. Five minutes later, she pulled her trusty Malibu into Alice's driveway. The heat was on full blast, though it barely made a dent in the cold. Her breath came out in clouds of fog that coated the windows in frosty patterns that reminded her of fine lace.

She honked the horn, waiting for Alice in the idling car. She hadn't paid much attention before, but now, after talking about the renovation and looking at the old blueprints, she noticed that her grandparents had done a remarkable job in converting the carriage house from a utilitarian building into something that truly looked like a home. The Swanns had chosen a different color scheme from Grey Gables with its white siding and gray accents. Annie made a mental note that when the carriage house needed it, she would suggest to Alice that it be painted to match Grey Gables, as she was sure it once had been.

"What could be taking that girl so long?" she asked aloud, just as Alice's arm snaked out the front door in a come-help-me gesture.

Annie unbuckled her seat belt and got out. She left the car running in hopes that it would finally warm up.

"Yes?" she asked, peeking in the front door. "Don't tell me you need me to carry you to the car!"

"I just need you to carry *this*," Alice replied, handing

Annie a plastic grocery bag and a Tupperware container full of cookies.

"You baked again!"

"I sure did! Another of the recipes we found," Alice answered as she put on her coat and picked up her tote bag. "Chocolate chip and oatmeal."

Annie got in the driver's seat while Alice threw her things in the back and then climbed in the front.

"Are you sure trying another of those recipes was a good idea?" Annie asked as they buckled their seat belts and she backed out of the drive. "We discussed this, considering the one you made last week didn't turn out well at all."

"Yes, I know, but I thought I'd try another one, just in case that last dish was a temporary blip in my baking mojo. Besides, I could read practically all of the ingredients and directions on this one. I tried one, and it's pretty good, if I say so myself!"

"You better hope you got it right this time," said Annie. "I don't need any of your bad baking vibes to rub off on me—not to mention what our friends will say. Though to be honest, I wish we'd recorded the looks on their faces last week. The horror! The disgust! In Stella's case—the how-in-the-world-do-I-maintain-my-dignity look!"

"You just *wish* my excellent baking skills would rub off on you," Alice said, punching her friend lightly in the arm. "There. That should do it."

"I'm not sure I really want it after last week," Annie said, brushing at her arm.

All the parking spots near A Stitch in Time were full, so Annie obligingly stopped to let Alice out near the door and drove down the street in search of a space. She found one in front of Finer Things, parked, and leaned into the backseat to retrieve her purse and tote bag. Alice had taken the Tupperware and plastic bag, but left her own tote and purse behind.

"Of course, Alice's purse *would* be on the other side of the car," Annie grumbled; she practically had to crawl inside to grab it.

"Hi, Annie!" she heard a familiar voice say as she scooted backward to get out, clutching Alice's purse and bag and her own belongings.

When she stood up, Ian Butler, Stony Point's handsome mayor, stood on the other side of the door, grinning at her. She felt her ears turn red, imagining the sight of her backside sticking out of the car, but thankful it was at least clad in a nice pair of jeans, as opposed to the shapeless khakis she'd worn the previous week.

"Oh! Hi, Ian," she stammered. "How are you?"

"I'm well, and you?" His polite answer belied the mischievous look on his face.

"Just grabbing Alice's things to take to the Hook and Needle Club meeting. The injury to her ankle has apparently spread to her arms as well."

Ian laughed. "That's our Alice for you."

"Indeed. I'd say she didn't care about others, but we know that's not true. She's just very dramatic—and occasionally forgetful." Annie paused. "Sorry, but I've got to run. I'm late for the meeting."

"What are you doing afterwards?" asked Ian. "Care to join me at The Cup & Saucer for lunch?"

"Why, yes. I'd love to," Annie replied without thinking.

"See you in about an hour, then." He smiled and headed across the street toward Town Hall.

Annie watched him walk away and noted that he was attractive from the front *and* the back. Then she chided herself for even thinking such thoughts about the man. Ian was just a friend, nothing more. Or was he? They had gone on a few dates, but lunch at The Cup & Saucer wouldn't count as a date. A date would be at Maplehurst Inn or Lilia's Tea House. But The Cup & Saucer? That would be just two friends eating lunch together. Right?

Who was Annie kidding? She glanced at Ian again, now headed through the front doors of Town Hall. She knew—spoken or unspoken—that they were becoming more than "just friends."

Annie finally shook off her thoughts of Ian and walked to the corner of Oak Lane and Main Street and across to A Stitch in Time. The meeting was in full swing when she walked in the door. Her friends sat in their favorite spots and worked away on their various pieces, chatting away and eating cookies. Annie stuffed her scarf and gloves into the pockets of her coat, took it off, and hung it on the rack. She found an empty chair and plunked down in it, placing all of the various bags on the floor next to her feet.

"Alice, you left your tote and your purse in my car," she called, pulling out her yarn and crochet hook.

"I knew you'd bring them in for me," her friend responded. "Care to try a cookie? As you can tell, these turned out perfect!"

"They really did," said Kate. "These are probably the

best cookies I've ever eaten. And those came from the same mysterious cache of recipes as that dish from last week? Amazing!"

The other ladies murmured in agreement.

"They are delicious," said Stella, brushing an imaginary crumb off her houndstooth jacket. "Alice, may I save a few for Jason?"

"Absolutely!" she said jubilantly. "See, I told you Annie. Last week's mishap was a mere anomaly."

Annie passed Alice's tote to Alice, and Alice passed the cookies to Annie. She took out two cookies and bit into one.

"Wow, you're right. This is very tasty," she said, avoiding Alice's look of triumph.

"Now that Annie is finally here, we can begin our meeting," Mary Beth said, putting down her knitting and looking around the room. "What is everyone working on? Kate is rather anxious that we not let down Reverend Wallace and the mission trip."

Each woman in turn showed the progress she'd made on her work. They raved over Mary Beth's pretty yarn, and teased Annie about her tiny square. "I think the people in Haiti are the same size as us," Peggy said, a grin pulling at the corner of her mouth.

"Very funny. I'm using two granny-square patterns, and this is just one of the forty-eight squares," Annie replied. "Once I've crocheted two or three squares, I can pretty much make the rest without even thinking about it. I figured it would be easy enough to make twenty-four of two stitch patterns and then stitch them together."

Peggy was the last to share her project—a green and

white quilt made of light cotton in a simple triangle pattern. Everyone agreed it would be very pretty once completed.

"I've been wondering about something," Peggy said. She wore a white cardigan over her pink Cup & Saucer uniform and a pair of comfortable-looking white tennis shoes. "Isn't Haiti a tropical island, so wouldn't it be warm there? Do they even need blankets?"

"Good question, Peggy!" Kate set her crochet aside and faced the group. "I talked with Reverend Wallace at length about the trip. Yes, Haiti is an island, but it does get cool at night. And I looked it up—average high temperature is ninety-five, and average low is about seventy-two. It may not seem like much difference, but apparently seventy-two can feel cold when you're used to it being much warmer."

Annie remembered what a shock it had been to her system when she moved from Brookfield, Texas, to Stony Point, Maine. It rarely got below freezing in Texas, let alone have all that snow or the cold wind from the ocean. Someone had told her that the temperature in Stony Point had once fallen to negative thirty-nine degrees Fahrenheit. She shivered just thinking about it. And Texas certainly got *much* hotter than Maine—high temps in her new hometown would be around eighty degrees, while ninety-five was more the norm in Texas. So she could relate.

"Plus, the orphanage uses any funds they get to purchase medicines and food," Kate added. "Everything's donated; their government has been corrupt and ineffective, so it doesn't support the many orphanages on the island."

"I would guess there's not much money left over for

articles like blankets or other bedding, or anything else for that matter," Stella said, looking over the top of her glasses.

"That's exactly what the Reverend told me," Kate replied. "He said many of the children have nothing of their own. He called me a couple days after I visited him and told me that the orphanage director—whose name I have completely forgotten—was thrilled with the thought of giving each child a blanket they could keep. It would be both useful and personal."

"What about Annie's idea to make blankets for the people working there?" Mary Beth asked. "And how many would they need?"

"I knew you guys would have questions, so I took some notes." Kate got up and went to rummage around behind the counter and pulled out her notebook, flipping to the correct page. "Let's see, the director—oh, his name is Father Bruno—said about twenty people work there at any given time, but most of them are temporary volunteers. They could use a variety of blankets and share as needed."

"So the workers would use a blanket during their stay, and the kids could take a blanket with them if they get adopted or find another home, is that right?" Gwen asked. Her knitting needles flashed as she worked on a butter yellow blanket.

"Yes, exactly. And since it doesn't get very cold there, they don't really need heavy winter blankets like we use here in Maine. So hopefully no one is arm-deep in wool."

"Nope! But I was arm-deep in flour earlier," Alice quipped, to everyone's laughter.

"I'm volunteering the store as a drop-off point," Mary

Beth said. She handed each member a small stack of flyers copied on different colors of paper. "I'm counting on you Hook and Needle Club ladies to put these up everywhere you go."

She paused for a moment and then added, "Didn't Vanessa and Mackenzie do a great job decorating the collection box and creating the flyers and poster to track our progress?"

In her haste and embarrassment over Ian, Annie hadn't even noticed the big, colorful box on the floor next to the register or the tall poster taped to the wall just inside the door.

"That's not a hundred and twenty blankets on the tracking poster, is it?" Annie asked.

"Nope," replied Kate. "The girls said they didn't have enough poster board to draw that many. There are forty, so we can color one in for every three blankets we collect. I even brought a bunch of markers so customers can do the coloring if they want."

"If that doesn't get the attention of Stony Pointers, I don't know what will!" exclaimed Alice. "What talented girls, Kate!"

Kate blushed. "Thank you. They came up with the concept all on their own. And by the way, the 'Blanket Haiti' idea is from a company called Blanket America. They donate blankets to the needy, and they also have a mission in Haiti."

"Aren't those girls astute?" Stella said. Annie knew that was high praise, coming from the woman who wore diamond earrings to an appointment to get her teeth cleaned and who had started and now oversaw the town's Cultural Center.

"I'll put one up at the diner and hand 'em out to everyone with their check," said Peggy. "I'm sure Jeff won't mind."

"And I'll make sure John puts some out at the bank," Gwen chimed in. "He probably can't ask the tellers to hand them out with the cash, but he'll do what he can."

"I'll stick one in all of my Princessa and Divine Décor catalogs," said Alice. "And you know how those get around."

"Sounds like we're gonna blanket Stony Point too," Kate beamed. "Thank you all so much for your help!"

"Well, let us know if you think of anything else you need," Stella said. "Of course, I'll arrange for flyers to be posted in the Cultural Center as well. Perhaps we can display a few of the nicer blankets we make."

Kate clapped her hands. "That would be so wonderful! But how would you do that? Wouldn't it look weird to just have blankets hanging on a wall?"

Stella smiled and then said, "My dear, you leave it all to me and my capable staff. Remember, our first big exhibition focused on textiles. I'm certain we can come up with a marvelous display that will help promote the project, and of course, the Cultural Center and our fair town."

Peggy glanced at the clock on the wall and began stuffing her quilting supplies into her bag. "Oh no! I've got to get to the diner. The lunch rush will be upon us, and I don't want to be late."

Annie suddenly remembered two things: One, she had agreed to have lunch with Ian, and two, she was Alice's ride. She felt torn; she wanted to spend some time with Ian—alone—but she knew lunch with Alice would be extra fun. On the other hand, Ian knew she had driven Alice to the meeting, but hadn't invited her along.

"What to do? What to do?" She didn't realize she'd said

it aloud until everyone in the store stopped what they were doing and looked her way. "Oh, sorry. Just thinking out loud!"

Everyone laughed and said their goodbyes. Soon only Alice, Annie, Kate, and Mary Beth remained. Annie started gathering up her belongings as well as her friend's. The Tupperware container was completely empty of cookies. Not even a crumb remained.

"Um, Alice," Annie said quietly, sitting down in the chair next to Alice. She hoped the other two ladies wouldn't hear.

"Um, Annie," her friend replied in a whisper, "why are you talking so softly?"

"Well, Ian saw me getting our stuff out of the car and invited me to lunch, but ...."

"He didn't mention having me along, did he?" Alice had a mischievous twinkle in her eye.

"Not exactly ...."

"But he knew you'd brought me here, right?"

"Right."

Alice grinned, winked and then said loudly, "Annie, didn't you say you have some errands you need to run?" Alice could never understand Annie's stubbornness about Ian, and so she always spurred Annie to see him.

"Yes, as a matter of fact, I do." Annie tried to sound normal, but was certain she sounded like a bad actress in an even worse made-for-TV movie.

The look on Alice's face was now positively impish. "Well, dearie me, too bad my ankle is throbbing from this cold. And just when I thought it might be getting better." She twisted her neck around to look at the other two. "Mary Beth, Kate, do you mind if I stay here while Annie runs her errands? I just don't think I'm up to hobbling after her."

"You know you're welcome to stay here as long as you'd like," Mary Beth replied.

"Oh, thank you so much. I will sit here quietly and crochet on this blanket. You won't even notice I'm here," Alice said. "Annie, do be a dear, and get me a club sandwich and chips from The Cup & Saucer on your way back. There's absolutely no food in my house."

"I'd be happy to," Annie said. "Are you sure you don't mind me leaving you?"

"I'm sure. Be off with you!"

Annie gave her friend a quick hug; then she put on her winter wear and headed out the door.

~ 6 ~

*I*an sat at a table in the back corner next to the kitchen. *Thank heavens,* Annie thought. *Wouldn't want anyone to mention to Mary Beth or Kate or the others that they saw me here ... at least not right away.* Then she mentally chided herself again for being so silly. For some reason, that man sometimes brought out the giggly high schooler in her. Not to mention the embarrassed middle-aged woman who should be slightly more mature. Maybe.

She wended her way through the packed diner until she got to Ian.

"Why, if it isn't the esteemed mayor of Stony Point, Maine," she gushed, laying on her Texas accent a tad thick. "Are you all alone, honey? Mind if I join you?"

He responded by standing to pull out her chair.

"It would be my pleasure," he said as she got settled. He pulled a mock bow, almost knocking Peggy over as she came out of the kitchen carrying a tray full of food.

"Mr. Mayor!" she exclaimed rather loudly, cutting through the din of the restaurant and causing all the other patrons to turn their way. "You almost got clam chowder all over your backside."

"Clearly your extreme skill in the waitressing arts prevented such a calamity," Ian said, bowing again, to everyone's laughter. "However, if it had not been prevented, lunch—as you say—literally would have been on me."

"You'd better believe it," Peggy replied in an aggrieved tone. "Excuse me while I help my other customers."

"If you're not careful, Jeff will kick us out and ban us from ever eating here again," Annie told him as he sat back down and the other diners went back to their meals. "At the very least, our waitress might spit in our food."

"Nah," he replied. "Peggy is too sweet to do something like that. And anyway, I just did Jeff a good turn. I provided some much-needed entertainment."

"I don't know if it was *needed*, exactly."

Peggy stopped to take their orders, the now-empty tray tucked under one arm. "Shall I get your usual?"

"Of course," said Ian, smiling at her.

"Me too, but I also need a club sandwich and chips to go," Annie told her.

"No problem. Coming right up," she said, tucking a strand of hair behind one ear. She turned toward Ian and added, "But if you get in my way again, it might come right down on that pretty head of yours, even if you are the mayor."

"I will endeavor to stay out of your path," he assured her.

She smiled at him, whirled around, and went to the kitchen to put in their order.

"Peggy may seem sweet and mild-mannered, but she's really focused on getting her job done," Annie said, unwrapping her silverware from its napkin and placing everything neatly on the table in front of her. "If it had been me, I probably would have dumped that whole tray on your head."

"I'd hope not," Ian said. "And I hope she's back soon; I'm quite hungry today for some reason."

They sat in silence for a minute, the noise of the cozy diner washing over them—the clink of silverware, people talking, the sounds from the kitchen. The dark green ivy growing in the giant teacup planters hung down the wall, almost reaching the floor.

"So …." Annie started to talk but then trailed off. She wasn't sure what to say. After all, she had no idea why Ian had invited her to lunch.

"So," he echoed, unwrapping his silverware and putting the napkin on his lap. "I heard a rumor that you and Alice have a new mystery to solve. What is it this time?"

"Of all things, we found some recipes under a floorboard in the carriage house."

"Recipes?" Ian looked puzzled. "Just shoved in there?"

"No, not exactly," Annie said. She then explained what they had found. She dug around in her bag and pulled out the notebook where she'd scribbled her list. It suddenly occurred to her that although the club had eaten cookies made from one of the recipes, they'd not actually talked about the recipe itself or the mystery during the meeting.

"Here's what we know—" she started to say, but Peggy interrupted by dropping off their drinks.

"Thank you, Peggy," Ian said. "You always take such good care of me."

Peggy nodded, a slight smile on her face, and went through the kitchen doors.

Ian took a gulp of his drink. "You were saying?"

"Oh, yes," Annie flipped the pages until she came to the list, which she read aloud to Ian. "What do you think? Any ideas on who might have left the recipes?"

"Well, I remember the Swanns living there, of course," he replied, "but they didn't strike me as being very secretive." He leaned his face on his hand and looked thoughtful. "Now, you say the plank over the hidey-hole was different than the rest of the floor?"

"Yes, though I have no idea what kind of wood either one is."

"Chances are, the floors in both Grey Gables and the carriage house are pine. Likely whoever did the hiding would not have known—or would not have wanted to try to find out, for fear of discovery, how to match the wood."

"Do you think whoever it was might have come to the sawmill to get the new piece?"

"It's entirely possible, but that's something I have no way of knowing for sure." Ian smiled. "So tell me about your project for the Hook and Needle Club."

"It's not really *my* project—Kate came up with it. And that reminds me." Annie leaned down to dig around in her bag and came up with a handful of the flyers Mary Beth had given to everyone. "Would you mind putting some of these at Town Hall? We really want to get the word out—we've got to collect a hundred blankets. Kate's daughter, Vanessa, and her best friend, Mackenzie, designed these."

"No problem." He took the colorful paper and glanced at it. "Anything to help the Hook and Needle Club, not to mention promote the young talent in our town."

"Thank you. Kate will be thrilled," she said. "But I still can't figure out why everyone in town always thinks that I'm the only person who comes up with and does good deeds. Our little town is chock-a-block full of wonderful, giving people."

"Well, you always seem to get things organized and people ..." he started to reply.

"Here you go, Mr. Mayor, Annie," Peggy interrupted. "Enjoy your meal."

"Wow, Marie's fast today," Ian said.

"Your ham-and-cheese sandwich proved quite a challenge for her, but she managed to get it made," Peggy said in a rare display of sarcasm. "Annie, here's your tomato soup. I got you some cheesy bread instead of plain garlic. Let me know if you two need anything else."

After she had gone on to the next customer, Ian leaned over and said softly, "Guess Peggy has forgiven me for getting in her way—my lunch seems safely ensconced on my plate."

"I guess so," Annie laughed. "Lucky for you, Peggy isn't one to hold a grudge."

They were quiet for a minute as they started eating, and then Annie told him all about Blanket Haiti.

"That's got to be the Hook and Needle Club's most ambitious project to date," he said, polishing off his sandwich and the last of the chips. "Think you ladies will be able to pull it off?"

Annie groaned as she wiped the last bit of soup up with a piece of bread. "Well, we've got a few months, but I sure hope so. I'd hate to see Kate's face if we failed. It practically glowed while she told us about it."

Ian smiled. "I can only imagine."

"Oh!" Annie sat up straight so suddenly her knees knocked the underside of the table. The salt and pepper shakers fell over, and all the dishes rattled.

"Goodness, now *you're* gonna get us kicked out of here," Ian said. "Whatever is the matter?"

"Nothing's the matter. I just had a brilliant idea! Why don't you knit a blanket or two for the project? I know your mother taught you how to knit; Mary Beth told me so on our trip to the needle-art conference in Texas. She said you knitted a sweater for Tartan. You could be a temporary member of the Hook and Needle Club!"

"Me? Annie, I hardly think …"

"Yes, you! Or I can teach you to crochet. Oh, that would be great! There are tons of simple stitches you can learn, and I'm told I'm a pretty good teacher."

"I'm sure you are," he said, a twinkle in his eye. "But I don't know if it would be a good idea."

Peggy dropped off the check, picked up their empty plates, and asked if they wanted any coffee.

"Yes please, I'd love some," Annie replied. "Hey, don't you think it would be a great idea for Ian to participate in our project and learn to crochet?"

Peggy actually smiled at Ian and said, "That would be fabulous! You'd be welcome to attend our Hook and Needle Club meetings, and we'd all be glad to help if you got stuck."

"Well, I don't know …," he said.

"Aw, come on, Mr. Mayor," she said. "If *you* agree to

help, the rest of the town will feel like they should too! Think of the great publicity it would be!"

"Yes, Ian, think of the publicity!" Annie gushed. "I'm sure Mike would love to put a picture of you crocheting on the front page of *The Point*. I bet we could get something in the *Maine Sunday Telegram* and the *Portland Press Herald*. Maybe even a TV station would talk about our project! And of course, they'd talk about Stony Point too."

Ian threw his hands up in the air, mimicking a suspect who's been caught red-handed. "OK, I surrender! I'll learn to crochet and attempt to make a blanket to donate."

"Hooray!" Peggy said, leaning down to give him a hug. "I'll be right back with your coffees, and I'll have Marie make that club sandwich for you, Annie."

"So," Annie smiled smugly at Ian, "when should we start your lessons? I have plenty of yarn I can give you, or you can buy some at A Stitch in Time. Mary Beth is giving a 10 percent discount to anyone buying supplies for the project."

"Well, what are you doing this weekend?" Ian asked. "I thought you might want to go back to Sweet Nell's with me. It's been awhile since we've been there, and I had a lot of fun that time we went."

Annie felt herself blushing. There could be no doubt that going to Sweet Nell's, a karaoke restaurant in a former tire shop located halfway between Stony Point and Wiscasset, would be a date. She decided to revert to her Texas sorority girl accent. She picked up a napkin and began fanning herself.

"Why, Mr. Ian Butler, are you asking li'l ole me to go on a date with you?"

"Mrs. Dawson, I believe that is my spoken intention, yes."

"Bless your heart, Mr. Butler," she said, fanning more frantically. "I shall have to check my busy social schedule and get back to you."

"Please do that, if you don't mind," he said, grinning slyly. "You could give me my first crochet lesson before we go."

Peggy came by and handed Annie a brown paper bag. She gave her a huge smile when she noticed the older woman's slightly red face.

"Here's that sandwich, Annie. And thanks again, so much, Mr. Mayor. You both have a nice day, OK?"

"You too, Peggy. See you next week, if not sooner!" Annie replied.

Annie and Ian argued over the check for a few minutes, but Annie finally gave in.

"Consider it payment for the crochet lessons," he said. "I've got to get back to Town Hall. See you this weekend."

Annie sat at the table for a few minutes after he left, collecting her thoughts.

Peggy stopped by once more, a half-full pot of coffee in one hand.

"Let me guess. Our mayor asked you on a date," she said.

"How could you tell?" Annie asked, surprised.

"Easy. Your face is red, and you flapping that napkin about is a dead giveaway. And anyway, everyone knows you and Ian are sweet on each other."

"We are both too old for that kind of nonsense.

He's a very kind man and a dear friend. That's all," she replied.

"Yes, I'm sure that's it. You're just friends." Peggy grinned.

After a moment, Annie admitted, "OK, I guess it is actually a date. He wants us to go back to Sweet Nell's. We went there once before. And he agreed to let me give him his first crochet lesson that night."

"So that's what they're calling it now—crochet lessons," Peggy teased. "Sweet Nell's is so much fun! Wally and I haven't been in forever. It's hard to find a babysitter."

"I'd be happy to watch Emily anytime," Annie said. "Just let me know when. But of course it can't be this weekend."

"Of course not!" Peggy smiled. "And we might just take you up on your offer."

She gave Annie a hug and then added, "Kate and Mary Beth are gonna be so happy when you tell them about Ian!"

*   *   *   *

When Annie re-entered A Stitch in Time, Mary Beth was nowhere to be seen, while Kate was helping a customer with pattern books.

"Annie, how'd your errands go?" Alice called, stuffing her crochet work in her tote. "Did you remember my sandwich? I'm starved!"

Mary Beth walked out of the back room, sat in her favorite chair, and picked up her knitting.

"Sure did," Annie said, handing the bag over. Alice promptly opened it and drew out the sandwich, cut in half and wrapped in waxed paper, a bag of chips, and a saran-wrapped brownie.

"Hey! I didn't get a brownie with my lunch!" Annie said.

"I guess whoever put this together likes me more than they like you," Alice said, unwrapping the sandwich and taking a big bite. "I know I said I wanted to take this home, but I can't wait. I'm so hungry I could eat yarn."

Annie walked over to the coat rack and began the process of removing her scarf, hat, gloves, and coat. The worst part of winter, she reflected, was the constant bundling and unbundling that had to be done when going from one place to another. She'd wrapped herself up snugly for the short walk back from The Cup & Saucer and had still shivered the entire way from the freezing temperatures. Now she thought she'd pass out from the heat.

Mary Beth and Annie chatted while Alice ate.

Alice balled up the waxed paper from her sandwich, dropped it into the paper bag, and opened the bag of chips.

"That was quick," Kate said.

"Told you. Hungry enough to eat yarn!" Alice said around a mouthful of chips. "So, Annie, how *exactly* did your errands go?"

Annie felt her ears start to turn red.

"They went fine," she said. She hesitated a moment, then added, "Guess what? I ran into Ian at The Cup & Saucer when I got your sandwich, and he's agreed to take crochet lessons from me and participate in our project. He's also going to put the flyers up at Town Hall for us."

"That's awesome!" Kate joined the conversation, having checked out the customer. "I never even thought that any of Stony Point's men might want to help."

"I hope it's OK, but I told him he could be a temporary member of the Hook and Needle Club. Peggy thought it was a great idea too. She said if he participated, it would make lots of other people want to be involved."

"She's right about that," Mary Beth said. She shook out her blanket—it was growing bigger by the second—and eyed it critically, then began knitting once more. "Everybody in town likes Ian, and for good reason. Of course he's welcome to attend meetings. I'm sure that he's too busy to become an official member of the club, but we'll need all the help we can get to make our goal."

"I'm hoping we can get some publicity for the project," Annie added. "I know Mike will put something in *The Point*, and I plan to contact newspapers in other cities and the TV stations too."

"That would be so great," Kate said. "Thanks for thinking of it."

By now, Alice had finished her chips and eaten her brownie. She stood up, walked over to the trash can, and deposited her garbage.

"Annie, are you ready to go?" she asked. "I'm about pooped."

"No problem," Annie said, and she began the re-bundling process.

Once they were both in Annie's car and on their way

home, Alice turned pointedly to Annie and asked, "So, how was lunch with Ian?"

"Fine," Annie said. Knowing where this was going, she tried to change the direction of the conversation. "Did everything go OK while I was gone?"

"Nothing exciting," Alice said, "though I did make some progress on my blanket."

"Well, that's a good thing."

"Uh-huh. Unlike some people who go gallivanting at lunchtime instead of working. That reminds me—did you ask Ian about his cat, Banana?"

"Oh, phooey! I completely forgot!"

"Annie! I give you one job, and you mess it up."

"Don't I know it! But don't worry—we're getting together one night this weekend so we can start his crochet lessons."

"Just lessons, huh?" Alice cocked an eyebrow at her. "Nothing else?"

"Oh, OK, yes, there's more," Annie said, starting to blush again. "He asked me to go to Sweet Nell's with him."

Her friend laughed. "I knew it! You've got a date with Ian. You've got a date with Ian," she sing-songed as Annie pulled into her driveway.

"That's it. Get out," Annie teased. "And take all your junk with you."

"Fine. I'm going, I'm going," Alice said. She got out, opened the back door and gathered her belongings. "I just want you to remember that everyone loved the cookies—the very ones you said I shouldn't bring. I wonder which of the recipes I'll make for next week's meeting?"

Before Annie could reply, Alice slammed the door, waved and then hobbled up the front porch and went inside.

Annie just shook her head and drove home.

— 7 —

Wednesday, Thursday, and Friday ended up being very busy for Mary Beth and Kate at A Stitch in Time—even more so than usual, especially considering the season. Winter was typically slow, but neither one got to sit down much, and Mary Beth didn't make much progress on her blanket.

On Wednesday, Reverend Wallace stopped by the store and asked for copies of the flyer.

"How many do you need?" Kate asked, reaching for the small stack next to the register.

"Well, I'd like to put one in every church bulletin this coming Sunday," he replied. "So, about a hundred and fifty."

Kate's eyes got big. "Really? You want to hand them out to *everybody*?"

"Don't look so surprised, Kate," he answered, a smile on his face. "This is a wonderful idea, and the least I can do is help publicize it. Plus, the donated blankets will extend our ministry to the orphanage, even beyond what we had hoped to do and how we hoped to serve."

"Well, I figured you just wanted a few flyers to hang in the fellowship hall or something."

The minister laughed. "*That* I've already done. No, I want to make sure everyone sees it and shows it to their friends and neighbors. You know our membership includes people who don't live in Stony Point."

"Wow. That's—to steal a phrase from my daughter— super awesome! Unfortunately, I don't have that many copies made," Kate told him. "Would you be able to stop by later this afternoon?"

"Absolutely," he replied, rearranging his scarf and pulling his hat back on. "I'll see you later."

The bell rang as he left, and Kate sank down on the stool behind the register, shaking her head in disbelief. Mary Beth wandered in from the back room and noticed Kate staring into space.

"Uh, Kate? Is everything all right?"

"Gosh, sorry. I guess I just zoned out," Kate said. "Reverend Wallace wants *a hundred and fifty* copies of the flyer to stuff in every church bulletin this Sunday."

"Then I suggest you get busy copying, missy!"

"Yes, ma'am!" Kate saluted and then went to the back to get started.

*   *   *   *

By the end of the day Thursday, Kate had copied and given out more flyers than she thought possible. In addition to the ones for Reverend Wallace, she'd had to make more for the store—every single one had been taken. Then Vanessa had requested a few to put up at school. Katrina, the activities director at Seaside Hills Assisted Living, wanted to give copies to her, as she put it, "crafty residents." Valerie Duffy, one of the local librarians, asked for some to hand out to library patrons. Then Alice ran out of flyers and needed more for her catalogs.

And the stream of customers seemed to be never ending. They helped people they'd never seen in the store before, as well as regulars and those who hadn't patronized the store in a while. And every single one of them wanted to pick out yarn and an easy pattern and talk about Blanket Haiti. Kate began wishing for a clone, or at the very least, a recording to explain the project. Her jaws had started to ache.

In a rare lull that occurred late that afternoon, she plopped down on one of the chairs next to Mary Beth, who worked away on her knitting, and put up her feet.

"I ... am ... exhausted," Kate said. "I had no idea my little idea would get to be so *big*."

"Aren't you excited, though?" Mary Beth asked, pulling more yarn from her skein and turning the blanket to start a new row. "There's really no way just the Hook and Needle Club members could have made that many blankets."

"True, and I'm thankful that everyone is embracing the idea. But I'm worn out, and I'm going to have to order more yarn, pattern books, and colored copy paper."

"I'd say that's a good problem to have."

"Yeah, it is. But I'm still gonna wait until tomorrow to do it."

*   *   *   *

Kate spent most of Friday morning on the phone. She knew she could do the ordering online, but she liked talking to the sales reps. Many times they'd tell her about a new product or a discount that wasn't available on their website, and they often had ideas for things that would be good sellers at A Stitch in Time.

But first, she called the shop's office supply vendor to order more paper.

"Are you sure you need that many reams?" their rep, Gordon Richards, said. "I'm pretty sure that's more than you've ever ordered since Mary Beth opened the store."

Kate sighed, knowing she'd have to once again explain the club project.

She could hear him rustling papers around. "It's OK if you do," he said, "but it's my job to make sure our customers get what they need and that we don't have to deal with restocking unneeded product."

Kate sighed again and then said, "I appreciate that, Gordon. And yes, we need it. And yes, we don't typically use this much paper in a *year.*" She proceeded to explain the project to him, ending with, "and we probably need more toner too."

"I'll bet you do," he chuckled. "Tell you what. Let me check with my boss and see if there's anything on special we can get you. Like I said, sometimes we have to restock unneeded product, and he might be able to make you a deal."

"That would be great," she said. "As long as it isn't a hideous color or something."

Gordon laughed. "I promise. No hideous colors. Give me a couple hours, and I'll call you back."

Kate conveyed her appreciation and hung up.

She then called several other suppliers to order more yarn and patterns. They all assured her she could expect delivery by the end of the following week. Thankfully, none

of them asked why she needed so much, so she didn't have
to explain the project yet again.

She saved her favorite sales rep, Jenn Gracie, for last.

"Hi, Jenn, it's Kate Stevens," she said.

"Kate! How are you?" Jenn said. "What can I help
you with?"

"Well," Kate began, and she proceeded to explain the
project, actually happy this time to do so. She wished Jenn
lived closer; they had immediately hit it off and had such
fun during the few times Jenn had visited to show them
new products.

"Wow, Kate, that's awesome! I know I've said this before, but you totally are my favorite customer."

"Aw shucks," Kate said. "And you totally are my favorite
sales rep."

"Oh, stop," Jenn replied, laughing. "I mean, do go on!"
Kate imagined Jenn's long red hair tied up in a disheveled
bun as she walked around her messy office to pull out catalogs. She'd never actually seen Jenn's office, but she had
seen Jenn and her mussed-up hair and her messy car, so she
figured her office looked similar. By the end of the conversation, the order had been placed, and Kate felt like singing.

She'd just hung up the phone when it rang.

"A Stitch in Time, this is Kate, how can I help you?"

"Kate, it's Gordon."

"That was quick! Thanks for calling me back."

"No problem," he replied. "Listen, I told my boss about
your project, and apparently we've got ten cases of colored
paper—none of them hideous—that we can give you."

"Give—" Kate started to say, but he kept talking.

"You don't happen to have nonprofit status, do you?" he asked. "It's no big deal if you don't, but it sure would help us out if you do, since this will be a pretty substantial donation."

"Uh, well, no, the store isn't nonprofit, but the Stony Point Community Church is, and we're working with the church on this project. You could donate the paper to the church and get the tax write-off that way. I'm sure Reverend Wallace would be thrilled!"

"Wonderful. Be on the lookout; we'll ship them out as soon as we can, along with some toner. Have a great day."

Kate sat there, stunned, as Mary Beth came in.

"You will never believe this," Kate said, "but Gordon Richards's company is going to donate ten *cases* of paper to us to help promote Blanket Haiti."

Mary Beth's eyes got big. "Really? Ten *cases*! That's what—a hundred reams of paper? Wow! Where will we put it all?"

"Well, technically they're going to donate it to the church for the tax write-off, so we'll just use what we need to print the flyers, and the church will take the rest. But still …!"

The two couldn't help it; they jumped up and down and squealed like teenagers.

*   *   *   *

"Mom? Mom?!" Vanessa called as she ran into A Stitch in Time that day after school. The bell almost fell off with the force of her shove, and it continued to ding frantically for a few seconds after the door had closed.

"Mother! Where are you? Mom!" she hollered again.

Kate emerged from the back room, wiping her hands on a paper towel. She was surprised when her daughter barreled into her and gave her a big hug, coat, backpack, and all.

"Guess what?" Before Kate could even say "wha—," her daughter stepped back and continued, the words spilling over each other in a frantic effort to get out. "Mackenzie and I got an A on our project! And Mrs. Petersen had everyone get up in front of the class and explain their project, and then everyone in class voted on the best idea. And ours got the most votes! And a bunch of the girls—you remember Taylor and Lily, right? Well, they want to help, and so do Holly and Hannah and Avalee and Danielle, oh, and Tessa! Anyway, we all want to have our own teen Hook and Needle Club, but meet after school, of course, and all make at least one blanket, and I told them you and Miss Brock would be more than happy to let us meet here and that you would teach crochet or knitting. And then I realized that maybe I shouldn't have said that, like maybe it wouldn't be OK, so I ran over right after school to ask. But if it's OK, I'm supposed to find out what day we could have our meetings. We think Tuesdays, 'cause most of us have clubs and band practice and stuff that meet on the other days. And you guys have your regular Hook and Needle Club meeting that day too. But if it won't work, that would be cool too. You just have to tell me so I can let all the girls know."

When Vanessa finally stopped talking, Kate was surprised her daughter didn't have to bend over and grasp her knees to catch her breath, like runners do at the end of a race. She felt unsure how to respond—so much information had been thrown at her, and she couldn't quite remember the question. Plus, it would be her boss's decision, not hers. Just then Mary Beth came in the front door.

"Hey Kate! Oh, hi Vanessa," she said, unwinding her extra-long multicolored scarf from her neck, removing her matching hat, and pulling off her gloves. She then took off her favorite winter coat—a raggedy old peacoat that had belonged to her grandfather, complete with navy insignia and a patch with his last name—and hung it on the rack. "What's going on?"

"You just missed a speech of epic proportions from Vanessa—"

"Mom!" her daughter interjected.

Ignoring that, Kate continued, "—which I can summarize in about two seconds. I gather that a bunch of girls in her class want to launch a teen chapter of the Hook and Needle Club to help with Blanket Haiti, and they would like to meet here on Tuesday afternoons after school and get our help with crocheting and knitting. If it's all right with you."

Vanessa stood beside her mom, her face aglow with excitement.

She's so much like her mother, Mary Beth thought. *Same enthusiasm, same brightness of spirit.*

She pulled Vanessa into a hug and then walked over to the small display of Monster brand crochet hooks and knitting needles from indie crafter Yarn Rescue. Vanessa had been eyeing one particular hook ever since it had arrived. Mary Beth had discovered the artist online and loved her hand-spun yarns and whimsical one-of-a-kind needles with cute faces made out of hand-sculpted polymer clay. Yarn

Rescue was a one-woman operation, and she didn't make the Monsters very often, so each item in stock was extra-special.

Mary Beth picked up a hook with a pink head, spiky purple hair, and one big blue eye—she was glad that no one had purchased it—and walked back over to Vanessa.

"I dub thee 'Queen Boss' of the Teen Chapter of the Hook and Needle Club," Mary Beth said solemnly, touching the girl's shoulders with the hook like the old kings would do when knighting someone. Of course, she didn't plan on conducting all the rituals and vigils involved in a true knighting ceremony, and her black leggings and pink sweater hardly counted as special vestures, but her intent was the same. Mary Beth placed the hook in both of Vanessa's hands and bowed to her.

The girl bowed back, clutching the hook, and said, "Thank you." She looked at the two of them and then said, "So, does that mean yes? We can meet here on Tuesdays after school?"

"Of course, sweetie," Mary Beth said.

Vanessa squealed, jumped up and hugged Kate, and then pulled out her cellphone to call Mackenzie.

*   *   *   *

On the way home after the shop closed, Kate stopped at Sal's and picked up baked ziti and meatballs and an order of his divine garlic cheese bread.

Vanessa didn't even complain that she had to hold the boxes and bags on her lap as she sat in the front passenger seat of the car, or that it wasn't a pizza.

"Mom, this smells soooo good," she said, "and it feels great on my legs."

"I thought we could use a little treat to celebrate your A and your new status of Queen Boss," Kate responded with a little laugh. "Plus, there's nothing like a whole lot of calories to make a girl feel really good about herself."

"I know! And I can't believe Mary Beth *gave* me this hook," she said. She'd put the hook in her shirt pocket with just the head sticking out. "I love it, love it, *love* it!"

"That was sweet of her," Kate responded, glancing over at her daughter. On days like today she could hardly believe that she had birthed the almost-woman sitting next to her. It made her heart clench a little, seeing a part of herself walk and talk and have opinions and do such good things in the world.

"Can we watch a movie while we eat? I wouldn't mind seeing *The Princess Bride* again."

Kate smiled. Normally the answer would be no. She didn't allow eating in the living room, and she refused to have a TV in the kitchen; she wanted them to eat at the table like civilized people. But *The Princess Bride* was one of her favorite movies of all time. *And* they were celebrating.

"Just this once," she answered. She pulled the car into the garage, and they got out and began ferrying the food and all their bags into the kitchen. The phone rang as Vanessa set the last item on the counter. Kate grabbed the handset and managed a nearly-out-of-breath "Hello?"

"Kate. You haven't gotten back to me. So—can I have Scooter tomorrow or what?"

She stifled a groan. Harry. She had actually called him

a few times during the week, but had deliberately done so when she felt pretty sure he wouldn't be at home.

She took a deep breath and then said, "I actually tried to call you a few times, but I guess your answering machine isn't working."

"Oh, yeah. It isn't. I need to replace that thing. But ... whatever. Is Scooter available?"

"I just walked in the door. Can you give me a minute? I'll call you right back."

"Sure. But if you don't, I'll call *you* right back," he said, hanging up the phone.

She put down the handset, gripped the side of the counter, and took another fortifying breath.

"Dad?" Vanessa asked.

"Yup."

"Wanting to see me?"

"Yup."

Vanessa sighed as loud as her mother had, her pretty face clouded.

"When?"

"Tomorrow."

Vanessa's face brightened. "Oh well, I can't go then. Mackenzie, Lily, and I are going to meet tomorrow at the store to prepare for our first Teen Hook and Needle Club meeting. You know, pick out a few patterns and the right hooks and stuff, so the girls can just get started without trying to figure all that out."

Kate blinked, once again surprised by her daughter's foresight.

"I didn't know you three planned to do that!"

"Yup, we worked it out today after Mary Beth gave us permission. Didn't you hear me talking on the phone?"

"Well, yeah, but I didn't pay any attention," Kate replied. "Plus, you girls talk so fast I probably would have only understood one word out of three."

"Like Mackenzie says, you obviously understand more than you pretend you do. Anyway, call Dad back before he gets irritated and tell him I already have plans. You can tell him I'm free, oh, two weekends from now." She grinned slyly and added, "And if he remembers, I'll have something else planned then too."

"You are a bad, bad girl, Vanessa Rebecca Stevens," Kate said, picking up the phone and dialing. "But you're a girl after my very own heart."

*   *   *   *

Midnight. Kate knew she should be asleep, not reading a back issue of *Entertainment Weekly*. But for some reason she couldn't settle. It probably had to do with her conversation with Harry, along with the thought of her daughter growing up. She was already a strong woman, certainly stronger and smarter than Kate had been at seventeen. Soon her baby girl—who not that long ago had depended on her for absolutely *everything*—would be finishing high school and going to college, where she'd have to find or fix her own food, wash her own clothes, and get herself to class on time.

I'm not ready for that, Kate thought. *I want her to live with me forever and ever.*

The call with Harry had gone better than she expected;

instead of ranting and raving about "Scooter" not being available, he'd simply said, "Cool. See her in two weeks."

She had thoroughly enjoyed dinner with her daughter. They'd laughed and talked and recited lines along with the movie. Then together they had cleaned the dishes and put the leftovers away. It was the best night they'd had together in a while.

Even the snowstorm that had started while they'd been eating hadn't dampened their spirits. As Kate flipped through the pages of her magazine, her eyes finally got heavy, so she set the magazine aside, sent up a prayer for the continued health and well-being of her only child, and then fell into dreamless sleep.

— 8 —

Annie could not stay still for *anything* on Saturday. She tried sitting in the library to work on her blanket squares—she only had four blue ones left to make, and then she needed to sew the whole thing together—but she kept worrying about what to wear on her date with Ian. Her current garb, a grubby pair of jeans and her "World's Greatest Grandma" sweatshirt, was decidedly too casual.

The last time Ian had taken her to Sweet Nell's she'd been severely overdressed—not that it had been her fault. Ian had hardly given her a clue about the place; he'd just told her the name. This time, she wanted to look perfect.

She also fretted about teaching him how to crochet. What size needle would be best for him to use? What color yarn would he like? What type of yarn? Maybe Ian had a wool allergy. Or an allergy to synthetic fibers. Or an allergy to the metal used to make crochet hooks. *But that's silly,* she told herself. *He already knows how to knit. Surely he's not allergic to anything that has to do with yarn and crafting.*

Then she wondered if she could she find a crochet pattern simple enough for him to learn. She kept jumping up, running upstairs and looking through her yarn stash, trying to pick out some for Ian to use. She worried: What if she was downright awful as a teacher? What if this was the worst idea ever?

When not looking at yarn, she'd put various combinations of outfits on her bed. Dark blue jeans and a cream sweater. Light gray slacks and the same cream sweater. How about a black turtleneck under the sweater? Or maybe the jeans and a red-and-green flannel shirt over a yellow turtleneck? What about light blue jeans and a heavy wool sweater in various shades of green? Or ...?

She finally settled on a pair of jeans in a medium blue color and a green wool cardigan to wear over the red-and-green flannel shirt. She went back to her comfy chair in the library, pleased with her choice, and then she realized she hadn't picked out shoes or jewelry.

"Drat it all!" she said aloud, setting her yarn and hook back on the table once again. Boots managed the herculean effort of opening one eye, and then closed it and started snoring again. "Fine help you are, cat! I don't know why I keep you around."

As cats are wont to do, Boots didn't even stir, much less respond.

The phone rang as Annie passed by the table in the hallway.

"Saved by the bell," she muttered, picking it up and answering with a short "Hello?"

"Well, hello to you too," Alice said. "Whatcha doing?"

"I'm trying to figure out what to wear tonight!" Annie couldn't keep the exasperation out of her voice.

"Oh, right, your date with Ian," Alice said. She paused and then asked. "When is he picking you up again?"

"Six."

"Right. Six o'clock. So, if my math lessons from first

grade still serve me, that means you have *seven* hours until he arrives. Stop fretting!"

Annie started laughing—Alice always knew how to knock her out of a sour mood. "You're right. It's just, I haven't been on a date with Ian since ...."

"Since the last time?"

"Yes! Whenever that was. Seems like ages ago, even though I know it's not. And not that I have any reason to be worried—we're truly just friends."

"Just friends," Alice snorted. "You two are 'just friends' like Michelangelo is just a painter and Wally's just a handyman."

"Well—"

"Well, nothing," Alice interrupted. "I humbly apologize for asking this when your schedule today is clearly so— what's the word?—*grueling*, but would you mind coming over and helping me? I'm trying to go through some of the clothes I had in storage. I have no idea why I kept them, but since I did, I thought it would be fun to take you on a tour of 'Alice's date disasters' via my clothes."

"How can I resist such an offer? You are truly one of the world's best friends," Annie said. "Give me a half hour and I'll be there."

Alice snorted again. "Half an hour? You better be here in ten minutes. No more dithering around for you."

Annie could hear her giggling as she hung up.

Eight minutes later—Annie timed it—she had climbed the carriage house stairs and now stood on the edge of Alice's sitting room floor. That edge held literally the only clear space in the room; the rest of it, and the hallway, were completely covered.

"If I help you, you have to help me pick out something to wear tonight," Annie said, surveying the mess.

"Done!" Alice replied, not looking up from her spot on the floor. "Wally stopped by to give me an estimate. He said the only way he'd start to work up here is if I cleared out everything, and the downstairs does *not* have enough room, nor do I want to move everything yet again."

"Uh-huh."

"Yeah, and he also suggested we do the walls first in case paint or dust or whatever gets on the floor. He said it would be easier on him and cheaper for me in the long run if we try to do all the painting at once, and then the floors, and so on. We're going to try to redo the entire upstairs, all at the same time, which means I've got a lot of work to do."

"Do you really think you can go through all this?" Annie asked, flinging out her arms to encompass the piles.

"Sure, why not?" Alice replied, finally looking up from a pile of magazines she was sorting. "Winter's always my slowest time for booking parties. Luckily, Wally can't start working for a couple weeks—he's got a job in Bath or Bar Harbor or Brockton, or one of those that starts with a B. Anyway, I've got a little time. And I will be so glad to have this mess out of here. I haven't even looked at most of this since I moved in. I haven't used a lot of the stuff in my closets, and definitely haven't missed the stuff I put in storage, so why hang onto all of it? It will be nice to have a fresh start. Will you help me sort and carry boxes to the dump or the thrift store?"

"Sure, why not," Annie echoed, moving aside some junk

and sitting down gingerly on the floor. "What about having a yard sale when the weather warms up a bit?"

"Eeew. Yuck—no! I hate yard sales. You probably don't remember that Mom was a yard-sale fanatic—holding them *and* going to them."

"No," Annie said, puzzled. "I don't remember that at all. Where was I?"

"Oh, probably doing chores for Betsy, or sleeping. Yard sales are always super-early, which meant I didn't get to sleep in, and I hated it. But the best part? My mother would often buy things at someone's yard sale that she'd already *sold* at one of her yard sales, only to turn around and sell them *again* at—you guessed it—yet another of her yard sales. My sister, Angela, and I had to help customers. We lived in a constant state of mortification; people of course noticed—and talked about it. They probably had a pool on how many times she'd buy and sell the same item."

"Wow. I had no idea your mom was so … quirky. OK, we won't hold a yard sale. I'll cart your junk off instead, though I don't know that much will fit in my car."

"That might be a problem," Alice agreed. "We may have to get some assistance. Doesn't our fine mayor drive a pickup?"

Annie felt herself start to blush, so she ignored the question. "What happened to all of your mother's yard sale finds and inventory? Did she take them to your sister's house in Florida?"

"Ha ha. No. Angela and I went through everything, which believe me was quite the task and not a bit of fun. It took weeks and weeks," Alice said. "We each kept what we wanted and packed boxes for Mom to take with her. Then we had the absolute largest yard sale *ever*, only we called it an estate sale, which meant we could charge more money. Then we took what didn't sell to Goodwill."

"I think I'm beginning to understand your hatred of yard sales, and why your house is usually quite spotless," Annie said. "Anyway, I do believe you promised me a tour of your dating disasters."

"Indeed I did, and you let me know if there's something you'd like to keep for your very own. I won't even charge you. You never know what might strike your fancy. Like this outfit, the first on my dating disasters world tour." Alice held up a multicolored pantsuit. She proceeded to gesture at it as if she were channeling Vanna White. "I wore this lovely ensemble on a date with Malcolm Westley, circa 1985. Note the swirls of burgundy, purple, gold, and sage, and how well they complement the black. And we must not forget the bat-wing sleeves and of course, the monster shoulder pads."

"It's fantastic. Stunning even. Besides the outfit itself, what was disastrous about the date?" Annie asked.

"Ah, yes, the best part of the story. Malcolm took me to a club to go dancing. There he proceeded to spill my very fruity, non-alcoholic drink all over me, after which he left me at the bar, sticky, dripping, and mad, to dance with other girls."

"And why did you keep this outfit?"

"As a reminder of the date, of course." Alice said. "So, what do you think? Garbage? Goodwill?"

"Did you have it cleaned?"

"But of course! And I actually wore it on a few non-horrible dates too."

"That's good, I guess," Annie said. "How about Goodwill? I'm sure they have a section for costumes and what not."

"Throw it in the appropriate box, will you? They're the ones in the hallway." Alice said as she handed it over. Annie managed to chuck the outfit into a box labeled "Goodwill."

"Wow, I'm impressed," her friend said. "I had no idea you had that skill."

"Me either. I'm fairly certain I'll be getting up approximately sixteen thousand times this afternoon to put things in the right box, after I've hurled them into the wrong one. So, what's next?"

Alice shared the details of her date with "some dude named Romero," to which she wore a short, tight, white spandex skirt (Goodwill), which also got a fruity drink spilled on it; her date with preppy Knox Kingsley, which did not go well because she wore all black, including her eye makeup and scrunchy (shirt and pants: Goodwill; scrunchy: trash); and her date with Emmett Sadler, to which she wore brown cowboy boots and a long, multicolored prairie skirt with a white peasant top (kept the boots, the rest to Goodwill).

"You are a great tour guide," Annie said, wiping tears from her eyes after several hours of more dating stories. "I've laughed so hard, I'm crying and my abs hurt! And really? A guy named Emmett Sadler? Besides the old-man name, why didn't that work out?"

"Uh, well, because he *was* an old man—a friend of one of my college professors. I have no idea why I agreed to go on a date with him."

Alice yawned, and then looked at her watch.

"OK, don't panic, but it's four o'clock."

"Yikes! Time for me to get dressed!" Annie said.

*   *   *   *

Annie wore—at her friend's insistence, not to mention Alice's vehement rejection of all of her clothing choices—a pair of blue jeans embroidered with gold flowers down the left leg, and a cream turtleneck under a green knit cardigan with matching gold embroidered flowers. Gold hoops dangled from her ears, a gold scarab bracelet hung from one wrist, and she wore a pair of clunky brown boots with gold buckles.

Now Annie sat in front of her dresser while Alice fussed with her hair.

"Are you sure this isn't too much gold?" Annie asked.

"Gold is money, baby. And you look smashing."

"Even though literally none of this is *mine?*"

"Even so, even so. And you forget. The turtleneck is actually yours."

"Oh, gee, thanks. That makes it all so much better."

Alice stepped back to survey her handiwork.

"You look gorgeous, darling, if I do say so myself."

"Well, I'd hope *you'd* say so," Annie retorted. "These are your clothes and jewelry from Princessa, and you did my hair and makeup."

"Yup!" Alice replied, smiling and brandishing her flat iron. "Well, I'm off. You have a good date, you hear?"

"Yes, I promise!"

Annie surveyed herself in the full-length mirror, and then curled up in the library with her crochet work to wait.

She'd finally decided on a size G crochet hook for Ian—not too big and not too small—and some 100 percent acrylic yarn in a deep forest green.

The doorbell rang right at six o'clock.

"That must be Ian," Annie said to Boots, who yawned noncommittally. Annie gave herself one last look in the hall mirror, and then opened the door with a bright smile.

"Hello, beautiful!" Ian said, the big smile on his face mirroring her own. "These are for you." He handed her a bouquet of white lilies, lavender, and ivy, wrapped with a cream ribbon.

"Thank you, Ian," Annie said. "You are so thoughtful. Come in. Have a seat in the library while I put these in water."

"I wanted to get you your favorite flower, but then I realized I have no idea what that would be," he said, following her into the house and taking off his big winter coat. He wore a pair of crisply ironed jeans and a cream sweater.

Annie almost breathed a sigh of relief at her outfit. But then she worried that maybe they looked too matching. She'd have to ask Alice later. Or not. Her best friend would probably just laugh at her.

"Oh, I love all flowers," she replied as he went into the library and she continued to the kitchen.

Ian had settled himself in her grandfather's chair by the time she returned, bearing the flowers in a cut-glass vase. She put the vase on a corner of Grandpa's desk.

"Those really are lovely," she said, admiring them. "A girl always loves flowers, and they definitely brighten up the room, especially now when it's already dark out." She walked to her chair and sat down. "Are you ready for your first crochet lesson?"

"I'm not sure I'm up to the task," Ian replied, splaying out his fingers and examining his hands. "Other than knitting every once in a while—and I haven't even done *that* in quite some time—my hands are more used to manual labor and paperwork than yarn and—"

"A crochet hook?"

"Yes, a crochet hook."

"Oh, you'll catch on just fine, I'm sure," Annie replied.

For the next hour, Annie patiently showed Ian how to crochet. She began with the most basic crochet stitch of all, a chain. When he could do that well, she moved on to single crochet stitch. As Ian practiced, they also talked about the mysterious recipes. Ian told her he'd looked through some old records at the sawmill.

"Just as I figured, they were no help," Ian told her. "We have files going back decades on big orders, but I couldn't find anything about selling or cutting just one or two pieces of lumber. I guess they'd just put the money in the till and go on. Most of our work in recent years has been for major contractors. We haven't sold directly to many individuals in a long time."

"Well, you were sweet to look. Thank you," Annie said. "By the way, I keep meaning to ask you about your cat, Banana."

"Banana? How do you know about him?" Ian looked startled, and dropped his crochet hook on the floor.

As he bent down to pick it up, Annie laughed. "Oh, I just found Banana's file in with a bunch of my grandfather's paperwork. Why did you name your cat 'Banana'? And why did you keep doing things to make him sick?"

Ian grinned wryly and shrugged. "What can I say? I wasn't the brightest young lad. Now you know why I have a dog."

They went back to crocheting. "Wow," Ian said after completing a yard-long chain and then a row of single crochet. "I'm not doing too badly, am I?"

Annie smiled. "Pretty cool, huh? Making something out of nothing. Well, not nothing, out of yarn, but ... you know what I mean."

He laughed. "I do indeed. Very satisfying, this crochet thing. Like knitting, but obviously different." He glanced at his watch. "It's after seven. Shall we go?"

"Yes, absolutely!" Annie beamed. "Let me just get you a bag for the yarn and the hook, so you can take it with you and practice." She rummaged in the kitchen for a moment and returned with a brown paper sack. "And here's a reminder sheet about the stitches," she added, putting in the pages she'd copied out of one of Betsy's old pattern books.

Ian helped her on with her coat, put on his own, and then escorted her to his car.

— 9 —

*P*eggy sat next to Annie at the next Hook and Needle Club meeting. She leaned over and asked, "Did you have fun at Sweet Nell's?" Once again, Alice had baked one of the recipes, and once again, everyone raved about how good it tasted. But at the mention of the karaoke restaurant, everyone quit talking and swiveled their heads to stare at Annie. They started firing questions at her all at once, so much so that she had no idea who had said what.

"When did you go to Sweet Nell's?"

"Who'd you go with?"

"Did Ian take you?"

"Did you have fun?"

"I want to go there sometime. Is the food good?"

"You had a date with Ian, didn't you?"

The cacophony ceased when the bell rang as the door opened and shut.

"Am I interrupting something?" Ian asked in the sudden silence, taking off his parka and hanging it on the rack next to Alice's leopard-print coat. When no one answered, but a smattering of snickering ensued, he looked bemused and asked, "OK. What?"

Mary Beth regained her composure first.

"Ladies of the Hook and Needle Club, I meant to mention this before our esteemed mayor arrived, but Annie and

Peggy have drafted Mr. Ian Butler as a temporary member of our club, in order to help us meet our goal of a hundred and twenty blankets."

"And so, maybe, we can get on TV," Peggy said. "Annie promised to contact all the stations in the area. I for one would love to be on TV … I never have been!"

"And yes, so we can get on TV," Mary Beth said, giving Peggy a look. "But mainly so we can help those poor orphans in Haiti and assist Reverend Wallace and the volunteers with their mission trip."

"I could hardly say no to such persuasive arguments," Ian said.

"How wonderful of you, Ian," Stella said, her knitting needles never slowing. "You are very kind to help us with our little project. Have one of Alice's fudge bars. It's from one of those recipes she found in the carriage house, you know."

"Don't mind if I do," he answered, taking a piece from the proffered container. "And yes, Annie told me about the recipes. Of course, the fact that the hole was covered by a different kind of wood interested me. I thought maybe I could help solve the mystery by looking through records at the sawmill, but unfortunately, I didn't find anything."

"I didn't even think about looking at that plank!" Alice exclaimed.

"I'm sorry that it was a dead end," Ian said. He turned to Peggy and said, "Would you mind terribly if I sat next to Annie? She's begun teaching me how to crochet, and I'd like to continue the lessons with her, if you don't mind."

"Oh, no, not at all, Mr. Mayor." Peggy blushed a little, gathered her things, and moved to a chair next to Mary Beth.

"Thank you ever so much, dear Peggy," he said, bowing.

The blush gone, the young woman retorted, "Now don't you start with that again. You remember what happened the last time you tried that snobby stuff with me."

"Indeed I do, as I'm sure does everyone who dined at The Cup & Saucer that hallowed day."

"Which was what exactly?" Mary Beth asked.

"Come on, Peggy, help me out," Annie said impulsively. "Let's reenact it for them."

The two acted out the scene, with great embellishment of course, much to the ladies' amusement. Ian found himself laughing as well, especially when, in this version, the chowder actually *did* get dumped on him.

After their performance, Annie and Peggy bowed to the assembled ladies and took their seats.

"Now that we're all settled—" Kate began to say once the laughter had died down. She was interrupted by the bell over the door and the appearance of Mike Malone. "Now what? Are you here to join the Hook and Needle Club too?" she asked.

Mike look startled. "Why? Am I supposed to? No, Annie just asked me to get a picture of Ian crocheting for *The Point*. You know, to help publicize Blanket Haiti. Great name, by the way."

"Oh, thank you," Kate replied. "My daughter and her best friend came up with it."

"Nice," he said, barely glancing her way. "Sorry I have to rush, but I gotta get back to the store. Ian, Annie, would you mind looking this way please?"

The next few minutes were filled with "Ian, please

turn your head to the right" and "Annie, hold up your crochet a little higher" until Mike felt certain he'd gotten a
good photograph.

"Thanks for your time," he said, grabbing three of
Alice's fudge bars on the way out the door. Kate watched
him go and then turned back to the assembled group.

"As I was *trying* to say," she began, "we need to talk
about our project. First of all, thank you to everyone who
put flyers up around town. I think I've made more copies
in the past week than I've made in my entire life. There's a
stack on the register counter if you need more. And don't be
shy about handing them to everyone you encounter."

She paused dramatically. "And thanks to Gordon
Richards—our office supply salesman—his company is
donating *ten cases* of paper to the church so we can
make as many flyers as we need."

The ladies burst into applause.

Kate was determined to stay on track, so she continued.
"Secondly, I'm pleased to announce that we've received our
first blanket donations from the community. Valerie Duffy,
our very own librarian, stopped by the store last week to buy
a few things, and on Friday, she brought us three cotton
blankets. That means Valerie had the honor of being the
first person to color in one of the blankets on our poster."

She pointed to it—all the ladies turned their heads to
see that the blanket on the bottom had been colored a bright
green, with Valerie's neat signature in the middle.

"And Stony Point's favorite postal clerk, Miss Norma,
brought in *five* hand-knitted blankets yesterday. She said
she'd had them for a while because she ran out of people

to give them to, but kept making more. I had no idea she could even knit. So, as you can see, she got to fill in the next blanket on the poster."

Norma had used rainbow colors on her one and two-thirds blankets, but hadn't signed her name.

"That means we are up to a grand total of eight blankets; we still have one hundred and twelve to go. Can we go around the circle and share our progress on our own projects, please? Stella, would you mind going first?"

Ian leaned over to Annie. "When did Kate become such a taskmaster?" he whispered, making her stifle giggles.

Stella sniffed at the pair. With a flourish, she snipped yellow yarn with a small pair of antique silver scissors, tied the yarn into her blanket, and held it up with a flourish.

"Mine is complete," she said, to the oohs and aahs of the group.

"Beautiful, Stella! That means we're up to nine blankets!" Kate walked over and took the piece from the older lady. Bending down, she kissed Stella on the cheek and whispered, "Thank you." She then colored in the final third of the blanket that Norma had started.

"Voilà! Only thirty-seven more blankets to fill in it."

"You are quite welcome, my dear," Stella replied. "Ian's presence here has given me the idea to recruit Jason to our cause. He also knows how to knit, and unless I need him to run errands for me, he might as well sit in on the meetings as well."

Everyone looked surprised—Jason? Stella's New York born-and-bred driver, Jason? He could knit?

"Goodness. Don't look so shocked, everyone. I taught

him years ago as a way for him to pass the time when waiting on me. These days we do it together in the evenings
while watching the news and before we both retire for the
night. He might even have some blankets already made that
he'd be willing to part with."

"How wonderful, Stella," Kate managed to say. "OK,
who's next?"

Each member talked about their works in progress:
Alice neared completion on a pink-and-blue crocheted afghan; Mary Beth had only a few rows of purple left to knit;
Peggy's green-and-white cotton quilt just needed the edges
bound, so she'd started cutting squares for a blue-and-white
quilt; and Gwen needed to add white edging to her yellow
knitted blanket.

"Annie?" Peggy asked.

Annie held up a few rows she'd crocheted in a shell
pattern with green yarn. "I'm starting my next afghan—I
completed all of the squares for the previous one, and I
meant to sew it together this weekend but ..." She blushed
and then continued, "I ran out of time."

"Ian?"

The mayor held up his yard-long practice piece, to
which he'd added a number of rows in single-crochet. It was
starting to get lopsided, a common error for those learning
the craft.

"Almost done!"

Everyone laughed.

"And what about you, Kate?" Annie asked. "What are
you working on?"

"I just finished *this!*" Kate went behind the register

and pulled out an exquisitely crocheted blanket in rainbow hues.

"Why, it's beautiful!" Gwen exclaimed, looking over the top of her chic tortoiseshell glasses. "I'd love to have one just like it for myself!"

Kate laughed. "This is probably the easiest piece I've made in years. I wrote down the pattern for the crocheters if you'd like to try it."

Her statement was met with silence; Alice especially felt certain such a feat was beyond her skill.

Then Ian spoke in a serious tone. "I would like a copy. It looks easy, and I'm sure I'll have my blanket done by the next meeting."

"Thank you, Ian," Kate said grandly as the ladies laughed. She handed him the photocopied pattern. "It actually is a very easy stitch that only looks difficult."

"OK, fine. Hand one over here," Alice said. "I'd hate for the mayor to do better than an official Hook and Needle Club member."

"I'll take one, too, of course," said Annie. She glanced sideways. "You know, just in case Ian needs some help."

Kate winked and handed Annie her copy. "I'll have extra copies here on the register if anyone wants one.

"Oh, and I almost forgot—Vanessa, Mackenzie, Lily, and some of their classmates are starting a Teen Hook and Needle Club, and they'll be meeting here every Tuesday afternoon at four o'clock. If any of you have time and would like to stop by today and help out, feel free."

"I would love to, but of course I'll still be working," said Peggy. She looked a little wistful.

"Not to worry, Peggy. I believe my Tuesday afternoons are free, and I'll be happy to assist," Gwen said.

"Thank you so much, Gwen," Kate said, clapping her hands together. "Now, back to work!"

The ladies—and Ian—bent over their projects for the next fifteen minutes or so, talking quietly and munching on the fudge bars Alice had brought. Stella started a new blanket, and Ian continued with his practice piece. Suddenly, Peggy sat up, quilt squares falling to the floor.

"Hey! What about our mystery? Here we've been eating these fudge bars and haven't talked about the recipes hardly at all! And I don't think we talked about it last week, either."

"Thanks for reminding me," Alice said. "Annie and I made a list of what we know for sure. Annie, did you bring the notebook?"

Annie dug around in her tote, flipped to the right page and handed it over.

"OK. One—we found the items in a hole under a floorboard in the upstairs spare bedroom of the carriage house." Alice summarized the most important part of each clue, figuring that they would be there all day if she read every single word Annie had written down. "Two—the floorboard was a different wood than the rest, and no one noticed it all this time." She looked up at Ian. "Our kind mayor has let us know that the lumber difference won't help us solve the mystery. Three—that means the rug over it has probably been there for awhile.

"Four—we found a bunch of recipes in a mason jar, with a square of fabric, a spatula, a knife, and a bottle of spices. Five—most of the recipes are handwritten, and some of them are unreadable. They may have been first or second drafts of recipes. Six—a cook probably hid the recipes. Seven—the first recipe I attempted turned out terrible, even though the second one was delicious. And, finally, eight— Annie found the plans from when Betsy and Charles renovated the carriage house, and it turns out my spare room was the original bedroom, so our cook could have lived there as far back as Captain Grey's time."

"But not necessarily," said Mary Beth.

"No, not necessarily," Alice agreed. "Unfortunately it means we can't use that to narrow down the possible time frame. Nor can we use the recipes themselves, as they are all handwritten and none of them are dated."

"How many recipes are there?" Gwen asked, brushing off her navy blue pants.

Alice and Annie looked at each other.

"Honestly, I have no idea," said Alice.

"Since they are handwritten, and some are illegible, I don't think we ever thought to count them!" Annie added.

"You said they are handwritten. Is the handwriting the same on all of them?" Gwen asked.

"I hadn't thought of that either," Alice admitted. "Why do you ask?"

"Well, John told me about a fraud case they're working on." Gwen's husband, John Palmer, served as president of Stony Point Savings Bank. "Now, I can't tell you exact details—nor could he tell me—but apparently a customer had some checks stolen, and the thief did a remarkable job forging the signature. The customer swore he hadn't written the checks, and so the authorities brought in a handwriting analyst who could prove that the checks had been forged. The analyst even determined some characteristics of the forger that should help them find the criminal."

"Wow, that's really wild," said Peggy.

"I've seen specials on TV about stuff like that," Mary Beth said excitedly. "You know, where they look at a historical document and try to determine if it's real or fake from the handwriting and whatnot, like, copies of the Declaration of Independence. Maybe you should have the recipes examined!"

"I guess I could ask John who he used and find out how much the analyst would charge," Alice said.

"I've been thinking about this," Mary Beth said, putting her project on her lap, "and if I remember correctly, the Swanns enjoyed holding parties. The Swanns were *very* odd, and they served odd things at their parties. If you got an invite, you knew to eat before you went so you wouldn't starve to death—we called their parties 'culinary adventures.' So maybe the recipes you're making are theirs."

"But why would the Swanns have hidden recipes in their own home?" Kate asked.

"Maybe the Swanns didn't hide them," Stella said. "Maybe one of their party guests did. Someone could have done it as a joke."

"Why, Stella, do you know something about that? Were you at a party when that happened?" Alice asked.

"Of course not. Don't be silly. I didn't even live here when the Swanns did. It's merely conjecture." She sniffed and then went back to her knitting.

"So, maybe you should ask the Swanns about it, Alice,"

Mary Beth said. "Even if the recipes aren't theirs, maybe they'll know something."

"Well, I've been hesitant to get in contact with them," Alice replied. "I've rented from them for years, but I've never really dealt with them directly, just the company they hired to manage the property. I only met them one time when I moved in. Plus, I don't want to mess anything up with the negotiations to buy the place.

"Plus, to my untrained eye, the recipes seem older than that," Alice replied. "Best I remember, Betsy sold the place to them in the early 1990s. Of course, it could have been someone Charles and Betsy rented to, or even further back. We don't even know if someone lived in the carriage house during Captain Grey's time."

Peggy, dressed as usual in her waitressing uniform, had gathered her fallen quilt squares and put them in her bag. She looked at her watch, jumped up, and exclaimed, "Gotta go! Jeff will kill me if I'm not there to help with the lunch rush!"

"I, too, must bid you ladies a fond farewell," Ian said, getting up and bowing to the assembled group. "Time waits for no mayor."

Laughter ushered both of them out the door.

"However—and when—did you manage to make that beautiful blanket?" Mary Beth asked Kate as soon as the last Hook and Needle Club member had left. "And to write down the pattern too? Seriously, when did you have time?"

Kate smiled at the praise as she joined her boss in cleaning up from the meeting.

"I've actually been working on the pattern for a long time, and I used that weekend I had off to perfect it. I wanted it to look elaborate, but be easy enough for beginners. I actually got the blanket done in a week. *And* I only worked on it in the evenings."

"Someday, girl, you really must publish a book of your patterns—or rather several books," Mary Beth said. "I bet they would sell like gangbusters. And luckily, I know all the publishers."

"That is lucky! And how lucky am I that I work for the infamous Mary Beth Brock. I feel ever so special!"

"Oh, hush," Mary Beth teased. "I'm serious. You've got a talent for creating crochet patterns."

"Well, I don't know," Kate said. "I'm pretty busy between the store and Vanessa, and don't forget the article I'm writing every other month for *Hook and Needle Artistry* magazine."

"Well, if you do try your hand at books, just promise me that you'll include 'from A Stitch in Time in Stony Point, Maine' on every book."

"I'm pretty sure I can do that."

"Good," Mary Beth said as she finished rearranging the chairs.

"I hope the teen group is this neat," Kate said as she finished sweeping. "I guess we'll find out this afternoon."

"Do you need any help to get ready for that meeting?"

"No, actually, and *my* help isn't needed either. Lily, Mackenzie, and Vanessa apparently had a powwow on Saturday, and they picked out yarn and needles for everyone, and one crochet pattern and one knitting pattern. Vanessa said something about making it easy for the new members."

"Oh yeah," Mary Beth said. "I remember seeing the girls in here on Saturday, laughing and giggling about who knows what. It was during the time you used my SUV to take a bunch of boxes to the recycler. The girls had left before you got back. Did you know Lily is *driving* now, and has apparently done so long enough to carry passengers?"

"Yup. I guess she and her mom cashed a couple of those stock certificates that Annie had found in the attic to buy that car she drives."

"She just doesn't seem old enough to be driving. Cute car, though. Some sort of hybrid I think," Mary Beth said.

"Vanessa is old enough to drive too, but she doesn't seem very interested in learning."

"I guess not, since her friend has a car and doesn't mind driving."

Kate picked up more scattered plates and napkins.

"Did the girls make copies of anything? Or take anything with them?"

"Oh, I don't know. I wasn't paying attention. I had customers to tend: Joan McTavish and Frieda Stillwater. Oh, and Viola, Estelle, and a woman I hadn't met before. I think she said her name is Katherine. Odd that I'd never met her. She said that she's lived in Stony Point for a number of years. Anyway, I guess they talked Katrina into bringing them here for their weekly activity away from Seaside Hills Assisted Living. They're all sweet ladies, but God bless 'em, they wore me out."

"I don't know that I've ever been in the store when they've come in," Kate said, throwing away the trash. She grabbed a dust rag from behind the register and started wiping down the chair arms, the table and the counter.

"Count your lucky stars. Individually, they are sweet as can be, and I love helping them, but all together ...," Mary Beth said, mock-groaning. "However, in the good news category, someone had taken the Blanket Haiti flyer to the retirement home, and *that's* why they all came in—to get some supplies to make blankets."

"That someone was Katrina. She came in last week for some flyers," Kate replied. "I'm glad the ladies want to help, and that they brought someone new with them. They all do such lovely work. I'm so worried we won't make our goal."

"Nonsense," Mary Beth retorted, straightening some pattern books on a shelf. "It's just late January, so we've got plenty of time, and everyone is excited to help, even the mayor."

"Speaking of the mayor, is it just me or were he and Annie getting rather cozy? Even more than strictly necessary for a crochet lesson?"

"Nope, it wasn't just you. Everyone knows they make such a cute couple."

"Except for them."

"Yeah, except for them—well, Annie at least. And that 'we're just friends' nonsense Annie's always spouting—did you see how much she blushed when Peggy brought up Sweet Nell's?"

Kate started giggling. "I sure did. Hard to miss the red tips of her ears! Of course, we never did hear how the date went."

"Nope. Guess we'll have to ask next meeting," Mary Beth said. "I'd call her, but it's more fun to make her spill the details in front of everyone."

"And to see her blush."

"That too."

*   *   *   *

The rest of the day passed quickly, Mary Beth and Kate each grabbing a few minutes to scarf down their lunches in the back room while the other helped customers. Word *definitely* was getting out, and everyone wanted to learn more about Blanket Haiti. Some customers bought crafting supplies, while others dropped off checks or a few blankets. Kate happily got to color in two more blankets on their tracking poster.

In a rare lull, Kate ran out to pick up some snacks for the teen group—she knew how hungry growing girls could get. *And* they'd be more likely to come back if they knew they'd get something to eat.

Their FedEx guy surprised them with a delivery of yarn.

"I can't believe this is here already. I just placed the order this past Friday!" Kate exclaimed, signing his tracking device. "By the way, be ready," she told him. "I've got a *lot* more stuff on its way."

He laughed and then rolled his cart down the sidewalk to the next store.

"Let's see," Kate said to Mary Beth. She grabbed the box cutter and sliced open the packet on the side for the packing slip. She unfolded the slip and grabbed a pen to start marking things off. "Oh! It's from Jenn Gracie's company. She included a note: 'Best of luck with Blanket Haiti. I expedited shipping on this, just for you. No extra charge.'"

She grinned at Mary Beth, who said, "Well, quit gawking. Let's get this yarn on the shelves!"

*　*　*　*

True to her word, Gwen got to the store a little before the girls' arrival. She still wore her outfit from the earlier meeting, pressed brown slacks and a cream cashmere sweater. Her tortoiseshell glasses were perched on top of her head.

"Hello, Gwen," Kate called from the back room. "Do you need anything?"

"No, thank you," she responded. "Hope it's OK, but I grabbed the chair next to the window so I could capture the last of the light. The girls' young eyes don't need it as much as I do."

Kate laughed as she entered the main part of the store. "Of course," she said. "You can sit anywhere you want." She carried a tray of mugs, which she then put on the table in the middle of the circle of chairs.

"I thought the girls might like some hot cocoa and snacks," she said, returning to the back.

"Do you need any help?" Gwen called after her, but Kate had already reappeared, this time carrying a basket of cookies and one stuffed with bags of chips.

"Nope. I'm good. You want some cocoa?"

"Thanks, Kate—that sounds nice," Gwen said, smiling. "It brings back memories of my mother; she always had a snack ready for me when I came home from school. Cocoa is just the thing on a cold day like this."

She looked around, and then asked where Mary Beth had gotten off to.

"Oh, she had to go to the bank or something. Don't quote me on this, but I think she wants the girls to be set-tled before she gets back."

Before Gwen could respond, the door opened, and the room filled with laughing teenagers.

Gwen pulled out a fresh skein of yarn—this one was a pale green—and began casting on to start a new blanket.

Mere moments later, the girls were all seated, sipping cocoa and munching on the snacks. Vanessa, Mackenzie, and Lily had disappeared into the back, and then reap-peared. Mackenzie held ten skeins of an acrylic-blend yarn, each a different shade, while Lily carried copied instruc-tions for knitting or crocheting a blanket.

"Welcome to the new Teen Hook and Needle Club," Vanessa said. "As you all know, I'm Vanessa, but what you don't know is that I'm also Queen Boss of our club. Miss

Mary Beth Brock, the owner of the store, said that's what I am, so, uh, I guess I'm in charge—or something like that."

She looked around at the other girls in the circle of chairs and smiled. "And I'm pleased to introduce—if you don't know her already—Mrs. Gwendolyn Palmer. She's here to help the knitters. And you all know my mom, Kate Stevens. She will help those of you doing crochet. As you know, she's like the best crocheter this side of anywhere."

Kate smiled, and taking a page from Ian's book, bowed to the girls, who broke out in giggles.

"Oh, Mom!" Vanessa said. "OK, maybe she's the best, but she's also slightly deranged. Moving on, everyone knows Mackenzie and Lily, who are my assistant queens."

The two followed Kate's lead and bowed as well.

"So you two are deranged as well," Vanessa said.

"But aren't you supposed to bow in the presence of a queen?" Lily objected, giggling.

"We're not worthy!" the other girls stood up and started bowing as well.

"OK, fine. You can bow. Whatever," Vanessa said. "But let's get started. To make it super easy for everyone, we picked out one pattern for all the crocheters to make, and one pattern for all the knitters to use. How many of you are going to crochet?"

Four hands in the circle shot up.

"OK, Lily, please give Taylor, Holly, Danielle, and Sabena each a crochet hook and a copy of the crochet pattern. And of course Lily and I will be crocheting as well, so you can ask us for help in addition to my mom."

Lily walked around the chairs and handed each girl a

couple of sheets stapled together and a green metal crochet hook, size G.

"And who is going to be knitting?"

Three hands.

"Lily, please give Hannah, Avalee, and Tessa the pattern and their needles. Mackenzie will also be knitting. Oh, and please give Mrs. Palmer a copy of the pattern as well."

"I'm just learning, so I doubt I'll be able to help, but I'll try. Mrs. Palmer knows *a lot* more than I do," Mackenzie said, waving her pair of blue metal knitting needles, size 15, as Lily distributed the needles and pattern.

"Oh! I didn't realize everyone is going to make the same blanket. Thankfully I haven't gotten far on this one," Gwen replied, holding up what little she'd knitted.

"Oh, yes. The Queenies thought it would make it easier if each group made the same thing so we could help each other if someone got stuck," Vanessa replied. "Obviously the knitters won't be able to assist the crocheters, or whatever, but all the knitters can help each other and so can all the crocheters!"

Gwen nodded. "That's actually very good thinking." She took the pattern instructions from Lily and started reading the pattern to herself.

"Also, we figured everyone should have a different-color yarn—you know, so we can easily tell what blanket belongs to who," Vanessa said. "Mackenzie, will you please hand out the yarn?"

After a few minutes of clamor and laughter, everyone had a color they were happy with.

"When you run out of yarn, let me know and I'll get you

some more. Which reminds me, I almost forgot the most important thing! Our wonderful teacher, Mrs. Petersen, is sponsoring our club, like literally sponsoring it—she's going to buy all the yarn and supplies we need for the project."

Everyone started clapping and woo-hooing.

"I know, right? So, we all have to do the absolute best that we can to make her proud and so that she feels like her donation is worth it. But there's one thing—well, really, two things: she doesn't want like *everyone* to know, and she told me it's just for whoever showed up today. She wants me to keep attendance and a good record of what we use so she can pay for everything at the end of the project." Vanessa stopped and grabbed a piece of paper and a pen, and handed both to Mackenzie. "So, we're gonna sign in every week to help me keep track. Oh, and if you don't show up for 75 percent of the meetings, unless you have a really *really* good excuse, like a doctor's note or something, she won't pay for your supplies, which means you'll have to pay for it. So, any questions?"

A girl that Kate didn't know raised her hand.

"Yes, Avalee?" Vanessa said.

"Are you serious? Mrs. Petersen is for reals buying our supplies?"

"Yup! For reals! Any other questions?"

The bell over the door tinkled, and Mike Malone rushed in.

"Oh, Mike, you're back. Decide to join the teen club?" Gwen teased.

"Uh, no. Annie insisted I take a photograph of Vanessa Stevens and Mackenzie Martel with the blanket box. And she insists that I run it in *The Point*."

"Annie usually gets what she wants," Gwen said, chuckling.

Mary Beth came in just as Mike finished taking photos of the two girls by their decorated box and by the tracking poster.

"Oh! And here is Miss Mary Beth Brock!" Vanessa said excitedly to the other girls. "She's the owner of A Stitch in Time, and she's letting us meet here."

"Hello, Teen Hook and Needle Club members!" Mary Beth said as Mike hustled out the door. He hadn't even bothered to take off his scarf or coat.

"Hello, Miss Brock!" a chorus of teenage voices responded. "Thank you!"

"You are all so very welcome," she said. "Thank *you* for participating in our project."

"OK? No more questions? Good. Let's get started!" Vanessa said.

The girls rearranged themselves into two groups: the knitters surrounded Gwen, who began teaching them how to cast on, and the other group enthusiastically started making a chain stitch.

Everyone was so engrossed in their work—even Mary Beth, who had joined the knitting group—that the bell over the door startled everyone. The first mother to arrive, Mackenzie's mom, Sylvia Martel, stood just inside the door, shaking off flakes of snow. They'd been so engrossed that no one had noticed the fresh snowfall.

Soon Gwen and all the teens had donned their winter wraps and left, chatting and carrying their projects, patterns and hooks or needles. Mary Beth, Kate, and Vanessa were the only ones left.

"That went really well," Kate said. She walked over to her daughter and gave her a big hug. "You did good, Vanessa—really good. I'm quite proud of you."

"Yeah, yeah," Mary Beth chuckled. "Let's clean up and go home."

～ 11 ～

Thursday morning, Annie remembered the box that held the contents of her grandfather's desk, which she'd placed under Gram's desk in the library to get it out of the way—mainly because she bashed her knees into it when she sat down to email her daughter and some friends. She'd finished sewing together the blue-and-white sampler afghan the day before and figured she should catch up on her correspondence.

"Ow, ow, ow!" she exclaimed, rubbing her kneecaps. "Why didn't you remind me I'd put that box there?" she asked Boots, who of course lounged on the desk, her tail lazily smacking the mail and Annie's laptop. "Fine help you are, as usual," she grumbled, dragging the box out. "Guess I should do something with this."

She decided the easiest thing would be to call Carla and get her opinion, so she looked up the number and dialed it.

"Stony Point Animal Shelter," a cheery voice answered.

Annie pulled the phone away from her face and looked at it quizzically. Yes, she'd dialed the right number.

"Um, Carla?"

"Yes, this is Carla."

"Hi, it's Annie Dawson. You sound so happy."

"Well, I am! I just got word that all the shelter permits

147

have been approved, as well as our government nonprofit status!" Carla told her. "That means I can accept donations and apply for grants and be a part of animal-rescue networks. We can share ideas, adopt pets out to other areas, and even request transports from Pilots N Paws."

"That's wonderful news," Annie said, still taken aback at how excited Carla sounded. "But what is that pilot thing?"

"It's a group of pilots and plane owners who volunteer to transport animals to areas of the country where they can be adopted. I read about one man who has actually transported more than a thousand animals to new homes."

"Wow!"

"I know! I'm just beside myself to have all this done. Now I can actually do more for the animals." She paused, and then said, "I know you didn't call to hear all that. What can I do for you?"

"Well, you know that my grandpa, Charles Holden, was Stony Point's vet for years and years?"

"Yes," Carla replied.

"Well, I found a box of his old patient files, and I have no idea what to do with them. What do you suggest? You wouldn't want them, would you?"

Carla laughed. "Thank you for the offer, but no. I have *way* too much paperwork of my own to deal with. You could call a veterinary museum and see if they're interested. I don't know of any offhand, but I'm sure you could find one online."

Annie heard a chorus of loud barks in the background.

"Oops, gotta go. The troops are getting restless. I better

go see what they're up to," Carla said. "Thanks for calling. And good luck with that."

Annie ended the call and then sighed. She fired up the computer and looked up veterinary museums. Google came back with over thirteen million results, so she called the first one on the list: the American Museum of Veterinary Medicine.

A male voice answered, and Annie explained why she had called. "So, do you think you might be interested in taking them?" she asked when she had finished.

"Unfortunately, no. We would not find old patient files useful, and we don't have room in our collection for any. If you had old equipment, that might be a different story," the man told her.

"Nope, no equipment. Grandpa sold all of it when he retired," she answered, pushing her hair back from her face.

"Well, best of luck to you," he said, hanging up.

Annie sighed. "Now what, Boots? Should I go see Cecil Lewey? Not that he'll have room for these at the assisted-living center."

Cecil, a Native American of the Passamaquoddy tribe, had assisted her grandfather from time to time in his veterinary practice and had considered Charlie to be almost a brother.

Annie jumped up, startling Boots, who hissed at her. "But I bet he'd enjoy seeing them, anyway," she told the feline.

*   *   *   *

An hour later, she pulled into the parking lot at Ocean View Assisted Living. Even in winter, the views of the harbor from the hillside were just spectacular. She took a brief moment to enjoy the view, and then toted the box up to the reception desk in the large common room.

"May I help you?" The woman at the desk smiled at Annie. Her name tag read "Steph."

"Yes, I think. I'm here to see Cecil Lewey, if he's available. I probably should have called first."

"Oh, no, that's fine," Steph told her. "I can see if he's around. He usually doesn't take his nap until after lunch, and we won't start serving lunch for another 45 minutes. May I tell him who's here to see him?"

"Oh, absolutely," Annie said, placing the box on the floor. "That thing was getting heavy. I'm Annie Dawson. Cecil used to work with my grandfather, Charles Holden."

"Oh, yes, Annie! Cecil has talked about you a lot. Well, more about your grandfather, but it's very nice to meet you." Steph stuck out a hand for her to shake. "I'm Stephanie Thompson, one of the activity directors here. If you'll just grab a seat, I'll see if I can find Cecil for you."

"Thank you," Annie said, picking up her box and heading to a table near the window so she could take in more of the spectacular view. She had pretty much zoned out when she felt someone standing nearby.

"Annie?" she heard a melodious voice say.

"Cecil!" she said, jumping up to give him a hug. "I'm so sorry I haven't been by to see you in a while."

"Oh, that's quite all right," he said, sitting down in the chair next to hers. "I hear you gals at the Hook and Needle Club have been causing trouble again."

"What? Us?" she replied as she sat down. "And where did you hear that?"

He angled his head toward a bulletin board with a Blanket Haiti poster tacked to it. "Quite a few of the ladies are practically dying to come by A Stitch in Time to buy some yarn, but our van driver's been out sick and no one else has the proper license or something."

"Well, I could probably bring some yarn by if they need me to."

"I'm sure that would be appreciated, but I think they just need a field trip. We're all going a mite stir crazy. They won't let us walk the grounds in this weather, and who can blame them? Someone would probably break a hip." His dark eyes twinkled. "So what do you have there?" he asked, pointing to the box at Annie's feet.

"I found this in the attic at Grey Gables. It's chock-full of old patient files. I guess Grandpa made Gram pack up his desk in the carriage house when he retired."

Cecil nodded. "That he did. And he made her label it too. I don't think I ever saw your grandmother so cross."

"Why's that?"

"Well, best I recall, it was the day he sold off his equipment, so he was acting pretty cranky to begin with. Betsy said she didn't think he'd ever need the files again, so why keep 'em, and he said something along the lines of 'I don't think you'll ever need all that junk you've got in the attic either, so you can for dang sure find room up there for one tiny little box.' I had to stifle my laughter when each of them went away, muttering."

"But Gram went ahead and packed everything up anyway."

"Yes, finally," Cecil said. "For a bit there I wondered if their marriage would survive his retirement—both of them being so independent—but the next time I saw them, they were cooing like lovebirds."

"I love hearing stories about my grandparents," Annie said. "Even stories like that. Anyway, I found this box and didn't quite know what to do with it. Carla at the shelter said she didn't want it, and a vet museum said they had no use for old files, so I thought maybe you'd like to look through them. Of course, you don't have to keep them, but I wanted to give you the opportunity to see them before I recycled everything. Of course, if you *want* to keep any of it, you're welcome to."

Cecil laughed and put his hand on her arm.

"You are so very much like your grandmother," he said. "Tell you what. Why don't you leave them with me? I'm sure I'll enjoy looking through them, and there may be a few I'd like to hang on to. And I'll take care of the recycling."

"Oh, would you?" Annie realized she'd clasped her hands together like a little girl begging Santa for a very special Christmas gift.

"Yes, Annie, I will," he said, running fingers through his gray hair. "I'm sure I will thoroughly enjoy looking through these and taking a walk down the old memory lane. And some of the other inmates here might like it too."

"Inmates?" Annie laughed.

"Yeah, don't tell Steph, but we call her and the others our jailers." Cecil winked.

"I have another question for you," Annie said. "Do you remember anyone ever staying upstairs in the carriage house during the time you worked with Grandpa?"

"What do you mean by staying?" Cecil's face sported a puzzled look.

"Spending the night, living there, or anything like that?"

"Not really," Cecil said. "Your mother might have played up there when she was little, but other than that, I don't recall anyone ever really being up there. Your grandfather and I would use the bathroom on occasion, and seems like it was furnished enough that someone *could* have. But no—I don't think anyone ever really stayed there until Betsy sold the place to that couple from New York. Why do you ask?"

Annie told him about the discovery of the recipes and other items.

"Hmmm," he said, just as a bell chimed. "Well, that means it's lunch. It was so nice to see you, Annie. Come by and visit anytime. And good luck figuring out that mystery."

"I will, and thanks," she said as he pulled her into a hug and started walking down the hall. "Wait, what about your box?" she called.

He turned and smiled. "I'll have a jailer take it to my room."

*   *   *   *

"This is ridiculous," Annie said. It was Saturday, and she sat in Alice's sitting room, shivering under three layers of sweaters, a turtleneck, and a pair of leggings under some sweatpants. "Why don't you just replace the furnace already? I don't mind helping you clean and sort, but this is inhumane. There's got to be a law against such treatment, or at least the Geneva Convention! I'm freezing!"

"Yeah, yeah, the Geneva Convention specifically states, 'Alice MacFarlane is expressly prohibited from making Annie Dawson work where it's cold.'"

Annie responded by throwing a wadded-up skirt at her friend, who grabbed it and tossed it in one of the boxes that were now the bins for recycling her discarded clothing.

"OK, truth be told, I have a meeting with John Palmer on Monday to discuss this very issue. Since the Swanns are still the owners—and I'm still a renter—technically they're supposed to have it replaced. But since we're in the process of transferring ownership, and since I've been here quite a while, I'd feel bad if they paid for the whole thing. I figure I can put the furnace in with the house mortgage."

"That's all well and good, but right now I can't feel my fingers!" Annie whined.

"Fine. Why don't we take the mystery recipes over to Grey Gables, count them, and do all that other stuff that the Hook and Needle Club ladies mentioned? Would that make you happy?"

"Yes. Except I'll have to strip out of all these extra layers."

Alice grunted. "There's no pleasing you. But fine. I will

risk hurting my ankle again and make the treacherous walk to your house. But you're carrying the recipes."

*   *   *   *

"See, isn't this much more pleasant?" Annie asked. The pair sat in the library, drinking hot cocoa and munching on goldfish crackers.

"Yes, but I'm wondering when you reverted back to third grade."

"Third grade? What are you talking about?" Annie protested.

"Goldfish crackers," Alice said around a mouthful of them. "I thought only kids ate these."

"Well, apparently, and despite your vast maturity, you don't seem to mind. You can't even speak without spewing crumbs of them. Anyway, I thought they sounded good, so I bought some."

Alice swallowed, took a sip of cocoa, and then said, "Well, you're right. They're good. But as your best friend, I have every right to tease you."

"I can't argue with that logic," Annie replied. "Let's do some sleuthing."

They took their favorite positions, cross-legged on the floor, and spread the recipes around them.

"Have you got that notebook?" Alice asked.

"*Now* you bring it up, after I've gotten all comfortable," Annie said, getting up and going over to the desk where she rummaged around. Then she remembered she'd left the notebook in her project tote, so she had to go to the hallway. A few minutes later, she plopped back down on the floor. "Ready. Oh! And I forgot to tell you—when I took the box of stuff to Cecil Lewey, I asked if he could remember anyone staying in the carriage house. And he said no. So that probably narrows it down to someone who was there either after the Swanns bought it, or before my grandparents did."

"Well, that reminds me of something!" Alice exclaimed. "I've been thinking—if Betsy packed up the box of files when Charles retired, why would the blueprints for the renovation of the carriage house— which would be needed to complete it—be in that box?" Alice asked.

"I don't know. Maybe Gram just packed them away when everything was finished." Annie narrowed her eyes. She then told Alice what Cecil had said about her grandparents' fight. "I bet that's what she did, wanting to irk him a bit. I didn't pay much attention before—but that box did seem to have an awful lot of tape on it."

*   *   *   *

A few hours later, the recipes were stacked in neat piles and had been cataloged, thanks to Annie and her notebook.

"OK, so what do we have?" Alice asked. "Besides a terrible thirst, that is; I'd love some tea or more hot cocoa."

"You know where the kitchen is," Annie retorted. Then she grinned. "I agree. It's time for some tea. And perhaps some vittles. I'm feeling a mite peckish."

"Peckish? You know, some days I forget you're from Texas, and then you go and say something like that," Alice said, putting her arm around her friend's shoulders. "I wouldn't have put it like that, but I agree."

Alice sat at the kitchen table and looked over their notes while Annie started a pot of tea and pulled plates from the cupboard and food from the refrigerator.

"How's a ham sandwich sound?" Annie asked, putting bread on the plates and opening a jar of mayonnaise.

"Sounds great."

"That is great," Annie said, "because I've already started making it."

"I knew you could read my mind," Alice retorted. "OK, we've got fifty-three recipes. Of those, eleven are completely legible."

"And you've made two of those," Annie said, laying a slice of cheese on the bread.

"Yes, the chocolate chip oatmeal cookies and the fudge bars—which tasted awesome, may I remind you?" Alice wagged her finger in Annie's direction. "And twenty-three are partially legible—"

"Like the one you made that first meeting."

"Yes, like that. And the remaining nineteen are incomprehensible scribbles."

"Promise you won't even *attempt* those," Annie joked, putting some chips on their plates.

"I promise, though it pains me to do so."

"Thank you." Annie plunked the two plates on the table and turned to the stove to pour their tea.

"Of the thirty-four that I can mostly read, it looks like

we have eight dessert recipes, six appetizers, seven entrées, and thirteen side dishes."

Annie brought two mugs of tea to the table, sat down, and took a bite out of her sandwich. "But we don't know what all of them actually are, do we?"

"Nope," Alice replied, picking up her own sandwich and taking a big bite. "Yum—that's good." She took a big sip of tea and then added, "I'm only guessing on the categories based on the ingredients and preparation instructions."

The friends continued to chat as they polished off their food. Annie refilled their tea mugs, and they went back to the library to compare the handwriting on the recipes.

After a few minutes, Alice said, "I'm no expert, but some of these are definitely written by the same person. I'm not so sure about some of the others."

Annie squinted at the two she held. "And these look almost the same, but these marks look like they might have been added later, possibly by someone different."

Alice peered over her shoulder. "Yeah, they do. I hadn't even noticed that."

Annie heaved a sigh. "And we're still no closer to solving this mystery than we were before."

"Buck up. When I talk to John about the furnace, I'll ask him about the handwriting expert. Maybe that person will have some ideas," Alice said.

"I hope so. Because I'm slap out of them."

"Another Texanism," Alice said. "By the way, do you care if I spend the night? It's *really* cold at my place."

"Sure, and you can use this while you're here," Annie

said, grabbing a pillow from the window seat and chucking it her way.

Alice grabbed it, laid down on her side, and pretended to snore.

~ 12 ~

On the first Thursday in February, Kate stood in front of the tracking poster, her hands on her hips.

"Why are you glaring at the poster like that?" Mary Beth asked. "It really is a nice design."

Kate turned to her, still glaring. "Because it's already February, and we've only gotten seven more blankets since Norma, Valerie and Stella gave their nine, plus my one. And no one brought any to the Hook and Needle Club meeting this week. That means we only have seventeen total, and we have almost thirty-five more blankets to color on this thing. That means we need one hundred and three more actual blankets! In four months! I don't know why I thought we could possibly make that many!"

"Kate, Kate, Kate ..." Mary Beth put her hands on her shoulders and then drew her in for a hug. "It's going to be fine. We'll collect plenty of blankets. And even if we don't meet the goal, we'll still be doing good for those poor orphans." Kate felt herself start to cry, her shoulders shaking, and Mary Beth pulled away, holding her at arm's length.

"Aw, honey, why are you crying?" Kate kept her head down, trying to hide her tears, and felt Mary Beth leading her to the chairs. A tissue got pressed into her hands after she sat down. "What is it? Surely you aren't crying over the blankets. What else has got you feeling so down?"

The younger woman couldn't help it—she started to deeply sob. "It's not the blankets. Well, maybe them too. I'm just—it's just—I mean—". She stopped talking, too overcome with tears to continue.

"Whatever it is, you can tell me," Mary Beth said in a soothing voice. Kate felt her stroke her back, just like she'd do for Vanessa when she was upset, and that made her cry even harder.

"I'm sorry," she whispered, pressing the now-shredded tissue to her face.

Mary Beth handed her the full box of tissues. "Seriously, it's OK. Just tell me before I imagine the worst and start kicking some booty."

Kate smiled a little through her tears. Before she could speak, Annie breezed in carrying a couple of big plastic bags, stopping short when she saw Kate's distress.

"What's wrong, Kate? Why are you crying? Mary Beth, why is she crying?" she demanded.

"I have no idea, but I think she was about to tell me," Mary Beth said.

Annie plunked herself down on the chair on Kate's other side, dropping the bags at her feet. She didn't even bother to remove her coat.

"It's just ...." Kate blew her nose. "I feel so silly. But Vanessa has decided she wants to learn to drive, and she wants her very own car. And she's asked Harry to buy one for her. For some reason, I had no problem with her friends driving her around, but her own car? That means she's really growing up. She's never had any interest in having a car before."

"When did she tell you this?" Annie asked.

"This past Saturday."

"Kate! It's Thursday! Why didn't you mention anything sooner?" Mary Beth scolded.

"I don't know," she sniffled into another tissue. "I guess because I feel dumb. And I didn't want to start crying at work. And yet here I am, crying. I've been crying myself to sleep, and crying after Vanessa goes to school, and choking up."

"Oh, honey," Annie said. "I know exactly how you feel. I thought I would just die when LeeAnn went off to her first sleepover camp. I cried so much that Wayne joked that he should invest in a tissue company. And that was just *camp*. I had to keep reminding myself that all parents have to let their kids go sometime."

"And she's a smart girl to ask Harry for a car," Mary Beth said. "It's something they can do together that they'll actually both like: look for cars."

Kate started another round of tears. Mary Beth and Annie just looked at each other.

"*I* wanted to take her shopping for a car. I took her shopping for her first bra, and a dress for her first communion, and her Halloween costumes. And he—"

"We get it," Mary Beth said, interrupting. "You did all the things with and for her that a *mom* should do. Don't you think you should let Harry do this thing a *dad* should do?"

Kate sniffled some more and said, "Yes, I suppose so. He wants to do it this Saturday. She's excited. He's excited. And apparently he's been putting money away for years to buy her a car. Who knew? The man won't help me out when she needs new shoes, but he's been saving for a car. And apparently he's got enough money that she won't have a car payment."

"Well, think of it this way: It means Harry does care for her more than he lets on," Mary Beth said. "Let them have their fun. And let him pay for a car. You know Vanessa will always be your little girl."

"And you won't have to worry about her driving," Annie said. "LeeAnn could be so scatterbrained; I cringed every time she drove somewhere. But she never had an accident. And Vanessa is so much more together than my daughter was."

"It's true that she is very responsible," Kate said, drying her tears and finally looking at them. But then she noticed the tracking poster and started crying all over again. "But wh … what about the blankets?"

"Kate's worried we won't meet our goal," Mary Beth mock-whispered to Annie over Kate's head.

"Oh, Kate! Of course we'll meet our goal. In fact, I just stopped in today to drop off the two blankets I've finished so far!" Annie reached into one of the bags and pulled out the green shell-stitch blanket she had made and handed it to Kate. She then reached into the other bag and pulled out the blue-and-white afghan. "I finished the blue-and-white one a few weeks ago, but kept forgetting to bring it in. So here you go! Two more for the cause!"

She stood up, walked over to the poster, and grabbed a yellow marker to fill in the space. "There!" she said cheerily, signing her name in the area she'd filled in. "Now we're up to nineteen! I also stopped in to pick up copies of your beautiful crochet pattern. I promised the ladies over at Ocean View Assisted Living that I'd bring them some supplies. I think about six or seven of them want to get involved. I'm also going to give them a bunch of the yarn LeeAnn sent me over a year ago. I don't think I'll ever use it all, no matter how hard I try, and heaven knows you two keep stocking yarn I want to buy."

"I hadn't even thought about Ocean View," Kate hiccupped. "Mary Beth said that Katrina had brought in a few of the ladies from Seaside Hills, including a resident she hadn't met—her name is Kathleen, I think."

"No, I don't think that's right," Mary Beth said. "Maybe Katy?"

"I'm sure it will come to you," Annie laughed. "Anyway, someone had already taken a poster to Ocean View."

"Who? And why were you there?" Kate said, hiccupping some more and wiping away the last of her tears. "Ugh. I hate the hiccups. It's the worst part about crying. Well, that and the terribly attractive puffy eyes."

"I especially love getting a red nose," Mary Beth said, hugging Kate again.

"Crying is *not* fun, but occasionally, we need to let it out," said Annie. I know this sounds corny, but tears truly do cleanse the soul." Annie leaned in, smooshing Kate from the other side. She let go and leaned back in her chair. "I have no idea who put up that poster at Ocean View. I'd gone there to visit Cecil Lewey. You know he used to work with my grandfather. Oh, and I told him about the recipes, but he said he didn't remember anyone living in the carriage house while Gram and Grandpa owned it."

"So, that means we're looking at someone who lived there either during the Swanns' tenure or before your grandparents bought Grey Gables—right?" Mary Beth said.

"I think so. Anyway, Cecil mentioned that some of the 'inmates'—yes, that's what they call themselves—really wanted to participate in the project, so I figured I'd help them out. I meant to go sooner, but time got away from me."

"That's nice," Kate said, her voice muffled by yet another tissue. She managed a weak laugh and added, "I mean, not that they call themselves inmates, but that you're taking them stuff."

She jumped up, seeming to be mostly back to her old self. "Do they need needles? Will anyone be doing knitting? The girls picked out an easy pattern for the teen club to knit. Let me just get you some copies." She dashed into the back room and then returned and handed them to Annie. "And here's my card. Be sure to have them call the store if they need any help."

"And you be sure to call me if you have any more crying jags about your baby growing up. Or come on over to Grey Gables. We can cry together. My baby has eight-year-old babies of her own. How do you think that makes me feel?" Annie said, smiling. "All right. I gotta run. I can't keep the inmates waiting. I hear they start banging cups or something."

*   *   *   *

As Kate unpacked and stocked yet another shipment of yarn that afternoon, she realized she'd been more than silly to worry about making their goal. If just half the skeins of yarn they'd sold were used, they'd probably be able to put the blankets end to end and reach Haiti from Maine. Plus, as Mary Beth said, it was only February. The mission group wasn't leaving until June. And she felt better knowing that Annie had cried over her daughter going to camp. She couldn't imagine Annie ever crying over anything.

"Guess it's just a mom thing," Kate said aloud.

"What's a mom thing?" Mary Beth asked as she walked over to help Kate with the new stock.

"Crying over your baby getting older."

"I don't know personally," Mary Beth said, "but I think it probably is."

Vanessa barged into the store. Once again, it sounded like the bell would fall off. She chattered away as she dropped her bag behind the counter and shucked off her puffy pink coat.

"Mom, can you believe it? Dad is actually going to take me to look at cars, and he's actually gonna buy one for me! What do you think I should get? I *reeeeally* want you to go too, but that would be just weird because—well, it would be. But this almost makes up for all the terrible things he's done. What color do you like? I kinda like green. Or maybe blue. Oh wait, white. No, white gets dirty. Oh, hey, Mary Beth. So, Mom, will you look at cars on the Internet with me tonight? He's taking me to Portland because he says they'll have a better selection, and then we'll eat somewhere nice. I am so excited!"

"If you plan on standing there, the least you could do is help your mother and me with this shipment," Mary Beth said dryly when Vanessa took a rare break to breathe.

"OK, sure, no problem." She babbled nonstop until the store closed, and Mary Beth shooed them both out to go home.

"See," she whispered to Kate, "Vanessa is definitely still your little girl."

*   *   *   *

Kate got home from work at four thirty that Saturday afternoon. Vanessa and Harry hadn't gotten back from Portland yet. She wanted to call her daughter to check in, but she figured that was a bad idea. She tried working on a blanket—just a few more rows and her third one would be done—but she kept putting the crochet hook down and staring off into space. She tried to watch something on TV and got the same results.

She finally decided to give Annie a call. The phone rang quite a few times before Annie picked up, sounding breathless.

"Annie, it's Kate. Am I interrupting something?"

Annie laughed. "No, I'm just out of shape, and I ran down the hall to grab the phone. I was just taking a tuna casserole out of the oven when it rang. How are you?"

"Um—" Kate started to answer, but then she stopped, unsure how to go on.

"Let me guess. Vanessa's not home from Portland."

"Nope, and I'm going a little nuts. I wondered if you'd

like to come over and keep me company while I wait. I'd come to you, but of course I want to be at home when Vanessa and Harry get back."

"Of course!" came Annie's immediate reply. Kate felt a sigh of relief bubble up. "Would you like me to bring the casserole? I have no idea why I made it—clearly I'll never be able to eat the whole thing—but it just sounded good."

"That would be very sweet of you!" Kate felt her stomach rumble. "I just realized that I haven't eaten all day."

"Well, we have to do something about that!" Annie said. "I just need to do a couple things, and I'll be over."

Kate hung up and surveyed the kitchen and living room. She went into "company-is-coming" mode—straightening the books and magazines on the coffee table and putting many of them back on the bookshelf, flipping the couch cushions over, dusting the TV, and then cleaning up the kitchen and putting dishes into the dishwasher. The doorbell rang just as she finished setting the table.

"Annie!" she said, opening the front door. "Come in! Let me take that dish from you. And put your coat anywhere."

"I've always thought your home is darling," Annie said, shrugging out of her coat and putting it on the back of the recliner.

"Thank you! Vanessa and I really like it. Obviously it's not huge, but it's pretty cozy, and we both have our own space. Follow me—I have some tea brewing."

Kate headed to the kitchen with Annie's casserole dish and set it on a trivet on the counter. She then poured tea into two brown pottery mugs and put them on the table.

"I don't know when Vanessa and Harry will get

back. Should I put the casserole in the oven on warm, just in case?"

"That's probably a good idea," Annie said, pulling out a chair at the table and sitting down. She put a spoonful of sugar in her tea from the sugar bowl on the table and then took a sip. "Just on warm, though. I might have already cooked it too much, and I for one am not a fan of burnt tuna."

Kate laughed in agreement. She turned on the oven and then set the casserole inside.

"So, how are you holding up?" Annie asked after Kate sat down. "Have you heard from Vanessa?"

"No. And I don't expect I will. She's very careful to keep her parents separate. But I hope and pray they're having a good time, and that they have found a car they can both agree on. Do you know that my child actually does know how to drive? I had no idea. Harry took her after school yesterday to get her license, and she passed the test with flying colors."

"When did she learn?"

"She conveniently forgot to mention their driver's safety class at school. Apparently if it's on school grounds, the kids don't need a learner's permit, and the parent doesn't have to give permission. Of course, she could have gotten Harry to sign a permission slip."

Kate's stomach rumbled.

"Why don't you go ahead and dish up some of that casserole? I'm pretty hungry myself," Annie said. "Believe me, there will be plenty left when they arrive."

They had just finished eating when they heard a car horn.

"That must be them!" Kate exclaimed, jumping up and grabbing her coat. She ran outside, Annie close on her heels.

Vanessa drove up in a little blue Ford, followed by Harry in his pickup. Vanessa parked, jumped out, and ran to give her mom a hug.

"Mom! Look at my new car! A Ford Fusion! Isn't it cute? We had so much fun, even though we had to go like ten different places to find one we both liked. And you should have heard Dad haggling with the sales guy. It was pretty awesome. Come take a look!" She grabbed her mother's hand and dragged her to the car. "You come too, Annie," she called over her shoulder. Harry climbed out of his truck and leaned against the bumper, a big smile on his face.

She walked her mother around the car. "OK, so it's not brand new, but it's in practically perfect condition—it's only got about twenty-six thousand miles. I really wanted a two-door, but Dad made me climb in the back of a few of them and convinced me that it would be a pain for my friends to ride with me. So, I got the four-door sedan. It has a nice engine—"

"A three-point-five–liter V6, all-wheel-drive," Harry interjected.

"Whatever that means. It averages 25 miles per gallon. Dad even made them wash it for me," Vanessa said, giggling.

"Double wishbone front suspension, double overhead cam, and 160 horsepower," Harry added.

"Again, whatever that means," said Vanessa. "I can hook in my iPod and listen to my tunes. Climb in!" She got in the driver's seat, Kate got in the passenger seat, and Annie got in the back.

Vanessa turned the stereo up. "Doesn't that sound great?"

"Huh?" Kate shouted, reaching over to turn it down.

"I can really crank my tunes, Mom!" She leaned over the parking brake and gave Kate a hug. "Can you believe it? My very own car!"

"I can honestly say I cannot," Kate replied. "Annie brought us some tuna casserole. Do you want some?"

"Oh yes! I'm starved."

The three climbed out of the car, and Vanessa proudly hit the "lock" button on the remote.

Kate walked over to her ex-husband and gave him a hug—probably the first one she'd given him in years. "Thanks, Harry. You hungry? Annie brought a tuna casserole and there's plenty. You're welcome to join us."

Harry hugged her back, making her feel both wistful and happy. "Nah," his voice rumbled against her chest. "Had a big lunch. I'm off." They released and Vanessa stepped in to give him a hug.

"Thanks, Dad," she whispered.

"You're welcome, Scooter." For once, she didn't even roll her eyes.

*　　*　　*　　*

"All right, people!" Kate found herself clapping her hands together, trying to get the attention of the Hook and Needle Club at the next meeting. She felt like an obnoxious and demanding school teacher, but figured otherwise no one could hear her over the din. "Ladies, gentlemen! Let's call this meeting to order!"

The chatter continued unabated, so she sighed, put her fingers to her mouth, and blew an ear-splitting whistle.

That did the trick. "Thank you," she said in the sudden silence. "Let's call this meeting to order. First of all, Alice has baked another of the mystery recipes—some sort of bread—and is handing it out now. Please refrain from starting to eat it until we're done talking. Let's go around the room and share our progress."

Jason, attending a meeting for the first time, raised his hand.

"Yes, Jason?"

"Thank you all so much for wanting to include me. I've always wondered what Mrs. Brickson did in here, and I'm glad I finally get to experience it." Everyone clapped, and he continued. "I'm sure she's shared this with you already, but she taught me to knit years ago. I've found it to be a rather soothing pastime, and I'm thankful she shared her talent with me." He reached behind his chair and pulled out a bulging plastic bag. "I'm certainly not as skilled as Mrs. Brickson, but I'm happy to contribute these seven blankets that I've knitted."

Kate felt her face start to glow. "Jason! How marvelous!

Be sure to go color in two blankets on our tracking poster and sign your name!"

They continued around the room, and by the end of the update, six more blankets had been added to the box, and a total of almost eleven had been marked in on the poster.

"Annie, you told me you have something to share?" Kate said.

"Yes, I do," Annie stood up, blushing a little. Kate figured it had something to do with Ian sitting next to her. He'd actually attended every meeting, even though his crocheting efforts were not very good, and despite the fact that the ladies constantly teased him about it.

"I'm excited because ...," she paused dramatically, "we got a front-page story in the *Portland Press Herald*." She pulled a newspaper from behind her back and unfurled it. Everyone gasped and then started cheering. The article featured a huge color photo of Mackenzie and Vanessa helping two other teens with their needlework.

When the hubbub calmed down, Annie said, "I contacted them a few weeks ago, and last Tuesday they sent a reporter and photographer to the teen club meeting."

"We must frame that and hang it in here somewhere," Mary Beth said, and everyone agreed.

"Can we eat now?" Peggy asked. "I'm starving, and this bread smells delicious."

"Yes! Have at it!" Kate said. While everyone else starting eating the bread, she took the paper from

Annie, looked at the photo of her darling girl, and brushed away a tear. "Not only are you growing up, now you're famous."

～ 13 ～

Annie hummed to herself as she climbed to the attic to retrieve more yarn. When she'd gotten home after the meeting, there'd been a message from Cecil asking her to stop by Ocean View.

"Annie, sorry to bother you, but the inmates insisted I call you. Apparently, a few of them have finished their blankets and a couple of them need more yarn." His voice had droned out the list, and she had scribbled it all down on a scrap piece of paper. "I believe those are the demands for today. Oh, and we have lunch at eleven thirty, and nap time is at twelve thirty, so maybe you could stop by around two o'clock." Annie heard whispers in the background, him shushing someone, and then he added, "Anyway, hope to see you later. Let me know either way."

Boots followed her upstairs into the attic. Annie went to the dresser where she had stored some of her yarn stash and opened the bottom drawer. Boots jumped in the drawer as soon as Annie opened it. The cat then rolled around in the yarn, batting at the stray ends.

"Boots! That is no way to behave!" Annie chided as she removed the offending cat. Then she consulted her list and pulled out the requested colors, which she placed in an empty cardboard box. The phone started ringing. Annie ignored it, figuring whoever was calling would just leave a message. Boots stalked over to the attic entryway, sitting at attention and switching her tail back and forth.

Annie heard the answering machine pick up, but no message. Almost immediately, the phone started ringing again. She continued selecting yarn and dropping it in the box until she'd gotten everything that had been requested.

"What in the world?" she said aloud, as the phone rang several more times. She picked up the full box and walked past Boots and back downstairs. She checked her watch; it was twelve forty-five. That was plenty of time for her to make some lunch and still get to the assisted-living facility by two o'clock.

The phone rang again, but the caller had hung up by the time she got to the phone. She set the box by the back door, and waited for it to ring again. This time she grabbed it as soon as it began to trill.

"Hello?"

"Annie!" Alice sounded breathless and panicked. "You're there. Where have you been? Are you OK? Did you eat much of that bread?"

"Um, I've been in the attic getting yarn for the crafters at Ocean View."

"But did you eat much of that bread I made?" Annie realized that Alice also sounded like she'd been crying.

"I had one piece. Why? What's wrong?"

Alice had definitely been crying; she began to sob in earnest. "Gwen got taken to the hospital. She's really sick. She started vomiting as soon as she got home and couldn't stop. She said that her back started killing her, and her pulse was racing. She managed to call John, and he took her to the hospital." She paused to blow her nose. "John called Mary Beth, who called me. I'm here now. When you didn't answer the phone, I started thinking maybe you're sick too. One more minute, and I would have sent an ambulance to your house."

"Oh my goodness!" Annie steadied herself on the wall. "Do they know what's wrong? And why would you think I'd be sick?"

"Because of the vomiting. My bread might have given her food poisoning. I imagined you sick and not able to get to the phone." Annie heard her take a deep breath as if she attempted to slow the tears.

"Well, is anyone else sick?"

"So far, no." Alice started crying again. "At least not that we've heard. Jason and Stella aren't home yet, but we've talked to everyone else."

"Hang tight. I'll be there in a jif." They hung up, Alice still snuffling and blowing her nose. Annie picked up the phone, called Ocean View, and left a message for Cecil, telling him she'd have to stop by another day. She then put on her coat, grabbed her project bag and some granola bars, and sped toward the hospital as fast at the Malibu would go.

Five minutes later, Annie pulled up at the hospital. She recognized almost every car in the lot, including Stella's white Lincoln Continental, Ian's car, and of course, Alice's red Mustang.

She grabbed her bag and rushed inside toward the reception desk.

"May I help you?" a pretty redhead in a long-sleeve blue

polo shirt and khaki pants asked with a smile. Her nametag said "Tracey."

"Yes, hi Tracey. I'm Annie Dawson with the Hook and Needle Club, and I understand that Gwen Palmer has been admitted. Can you point me in the right direction?" She put a hand on the counter to steady herself. Her heart beat so hard, she felt like she'd run a marathon.

"Mrs. Dawson, yes, hello! We met for about a second when your group made the layettes for the babies a few years ago. There's a bunch of them already here. Mrs. Palmer's in the ICU."

"The ICU?!"

"Yes, the ICU," Tracey said, putting her hand on Annie's for a moment. "It just means she's getting the very best of constant care. They're on the second floor. Take a left when you get out of the elevators and follow the orange line. It'll take you right there."

"Thank you," Annie said, practically running to the bank of elevators to Tracey's left. When she stepped off, she could clearly hear Alice crying. *No need to follow an orange line,* she thought. *I can just follow the sound.*

"Alice, please stop crying. It won't help Gwendolyn get better any faster," Stella said in a commanding voice.

Annie turned left as directed and almost immediately ran into a knot of her friends. Alice flung her arms around her, still sobbing.

"Annie, thank God you're OK."

Annie patted her on the back and then eased her into a nearby seat. "Yes, I'm fine. So, does anyone know what's going on? Is anyone else sick? Where are Kate and Peggy?"

"Someone has to keep the wheels of commerce turning," Stella sniffed. "Kate is at the store, and Peggy had to work. Apparently Lisa or somebody has the day off, and Jeff couldn't let her leave The Cup & Saucer. But they're both well."

"And what about Ian? Where is he? I saw his car in the lot."

Mary Beth answered this time. "You just missed him. He had to get back to Town Hall for a meeting. He's fine. But you can certainly call him if you want. I'll even let you use my cellphone." Mary Beth winked, and Annie felt the tips of her ears go red.

Blast it! she thought. *Why do I always blush when that man is mentioned?*

"So, what's wrong with Gwen? Is it food poisoning?" Annie asked. As expected, everyone started talking at once. A nurse pointedly clearing her throat interrupted them, so they turned to look her way.

"Hi everyone, I'm Nurse Arabelle," she said. "I'm sorry I can't let you all in to see Mrs. Palmer. She's only allowed one visitor, and of course, her husband is with her at this time. We're still running some tests, and we're not sure exactly what is wrong. As soon as we know something, either myself, one of the other nurses, or her doctor will let Mr. Palmer know. He will have to tell you whatever he feels comfortable with. Privacy laws, you know."

Once again, everyone started talking at once. The nurse raised her hand to stop them. "I know you are worried about your friend, but we are taking very good care of her. And if you don't mind, please try to keep the noise down. We have other patients, and we don't want to disturb them or their families. There's a lounge at the other end of the hall, and we'd appreciate it if you'd all wait there. I'm sure you'll be much more comfortable."

"Thank you, nurse," Stella said. Turning to the others she added firmly, "We should follow her orders and head to the lounge. She's right—the last thing we should be doing is causing distress for anyone else." Stella, Jason and Alice led toward the lounge, with Mary Beth and Annie following.

"Wow," Annie whispered to Mary Beth. "Alice sometimes can be a drama queen, but that was over the top, even for her."

"I know," Mary Beth replied quietly. "I think she feels really guilty because she's certain the bread from that latest mystery recipe is responsible for making Gwen sick."

"Not the best bread I've ever had in my life, but it wasn't awful either. Plus, wouldn't all of us be having issues if it caused the illness?" Annie asked.

"That's what I told her," Mary Beth said. "Food poisoning usually comes on pretty quickly, so at least a couple of us would be feeling ill too. It could be an allergy to one of the ingredients, but I think the doctors have ruled that out already."

"How long can you stay?" Annie asked.

"Kate said she'd watch the store and manage the teen club this afternoon, so I'm here until we get kicked out, I guess."

They heard the elevator ding, and shortly saw a group of women heading toward them down the hall.

"Mary Beth, Annie, how is Gwen?" June Wallace, the

minister's wife, asked when she reached the pair. "Some of us ladies from the church wanted to come check on Gwen."

Mary Beth stood to give June and a few of the other women a hug. "The doctors are currently running tests."

A door down the hall opened, and John came out of the ICU and walked toward them. He was dressed in a suit and tie—he'd obviously come to the hospital straight from the bank—but he'd removed his suit coat, and his tie was askew.

"How are you doing?" June asked, giving him a hug. "And how's Gwen?"

"Thankfully, her vitals are steady, but they have no idea what has caused this," he replied. "As for me, I need to get a sandwich or something to eat. I never did get lunch. Would one of you ladies mind grabbing me something? I don't want to leave Gwen for too long."

Annie started to reach for the granola bars she had brought, but before she could even get them out, the church ladies held out covered plates. The sight made her stomach rumble, and she realized she hadn't eaten lunch either.

John laughed, grabbed the plate closest to him, and peeled back the plastic wrap. "Thanks everyone! Anyone happen to have a Coke handy?" He took a bite out of the sandwich. One of the women dug around in her bag and handed one over. "Here you go, John! I talked to your assistant, Allison, and she told me that's what you prefer to drink."

"Remind me to thank her when I get back to the bank," he replied. "Thanks again, ladies. I'm heading back in."

"Before you go, can you tell us what's wrong with Gwen?" June asked, her hand on his arm.

"The doctors aren't sure yet, so they're running a bunch of tests. She's nauseous and uncomfortable, has a fever, and is dehydrated. They're pumping her full of fluids right now. Hopefully we'll know something soon."

He turned and walked back to the ICU, closing the door gently behind him.

*   *   *   *

Four hours later, most of the Hook and Needle Club members still kept vigil in the lounge. Most kept their hands busy with needlework. Annie stayed as busy as she could with Alice still needing some reassurance.

"Are you sure it's not my fault?" she asked.

"Yes, I'm sure." Annie heaved a sigh. "If *all* of us were sick, then you probably would have been responsible. But we're not. You've baked bread that tasted better—that's probably the fault of that mystery recipe—but nothing about today's entry was toxic."

Annie loved Alice dearly, but the girl was presently plucking at her very last nerve.

A little after five o'clock, John came into the lounge, looking tired, followed by a woman in a doctor's coat.

"Hello everyone, I'm Dr. Shay Barnett," she said, tucking a strand of long brown hair behind one ear and looking at a clipboard. "Mr. Palmer has given me permission to speak directly to you all. I'm pleased to let you know that Mrs. Palmer has acute pancreatitis caused by gallstones."

At first there were murmurs of relief heard through the group, but then the diagnosis sunk in. Gwen's friends all began to press forward with questions for the doctor about the condition and what would happen next.

"We'll keep her hooked up to lots of fluids and antibiotics, and in a day or two, when she's stable, we'll do surgery to remove her gallbladder and the stones," the doctor reassured them. "After that, we'll keep her for another day or two. Now, please excuse me; I need to attend to other patients."

John turned to the group and said in a hoarse voice, "I cannot thank you all enough for sitting here and waiting with me. Gwen's sleeping now, but I'm going to go back to her room so I'm there when she wakes up. I've called our kids and their families. Why doesn't everyone go home now and get some rest? Gwen's going to be fine, and I will make sure you know her progress and when the operation is going to occur." He turned and followed Dr. Barnett out of the room.

By the time the group had begun to disperse, Kate and Vanessa arrived, bearing a bouquet of lilies in a vase.

"I think I remember Gwen saying once that these are her favorite," Kate said. She sighed and plopped on a chair next to Annie. "How is she?"

After Annie filled in Kate and Vanessa on Gwen's condition, she asked, "And how was the Teen Hook and Needle Club meeting?"

"Well," Vanessa answered with a sigh. "We didn't get much work done, but we made a card for Mrs. Palmer and everyone signed it." She pulled a sheaf of multicolored papers from her bag.

"That's one card?" Annie laughed.

"Yes, it's one *big* card," Vanessa answered, "but I'm not sure what to do with it now, or how to make sure Mrs. Palmer sees it."

A nurse overheard Vanessa and walked over to where they sat.

"I'd be happy to pass that along to her husband," he said. "As soon as Mrs. Palmer is transferred to a regular room, we can put it up on her board." He took the sheets from the teenager. "Also," he added, "you might want to let everyone know that we offer a free service where friends and family can go on our website to send a card; we print them out and hang them in the patient's room. Let me know if you need anything else."

Before Kate or Annie could say anything, he had left, and Vanessa had whipped out her cellphone.

After a few minutes of pushing buttons, she said, "OK, I've sent a text to all my friends and told them they have to send a card. I told them they need to let all their friends know."

Annie stood up and stretched.

"I don't know about y'all, but I'm beat. I'm going home too. I'll see everyone soon."

*   *   *   *

A day after she'd been admitted, Gwen sat up and demanded that someone bring her supplies so she could work on her blanket. Despite being hooked up to IVs and monitors and being on painkillers, and despite her doctor's opposition, she knitted as much as she could while awake.

John reported that she had said she was still going to do her part, even if she *was* sick.

So many cards had been sent, the board was four and five layers deep and they'd run out of pushpins.

After two days, the doctors determined Gwen to be well enough for surgery. A large group assembled in the operating room lounge to pray, and then cheered when they were told that Gwen was awake and being moved from recovery to a regular room.

Two days later, Gwen got to go home.

— 14 —

nnie and Alice had spent the rest of February focused on doing three things: First, with others they helped out Gwen around Wedgewood, the Palmers' home, since John had to go back to work, and Gwen needed to take it easy. A week after going home, Gwen was pretty much back to normal and her cadre of volunteers were able to slowly wean themselves away from Wedgewood.

Second, Alice's Princessa jewelry sales and parties had picked up around Valentine's Day, but she and Annie still found time to finish getting ready for Wally to start the remodeling work on the carriage house. Alice and the Swanns had worked out an amicable resolution for the furnace issue, and it had been replaced, much to Annie's relief. It was also much easier to help sort out clothing and haul it away when she could feel her fingers. John Palmer and the staff at the Stony Point Savings Bank had finished work on Alice's mortgage, and now she— and the bank—would own the carriage house. All that was left was the signing of the documents and the loan closing.

The remainder of the time, Annie, Alice, and many other Stony Pointers were knitting, crocheting, and quilting frantically to meet their goal for the Blanket Haiti project.

March ushered in ... absolutely nothing. It wasn't really winter any more, but it was still too early for spring. High temperatures were only about forty degrees, and nights were still pretty cold. Snow still blanketed the Maine countryside, looking like a picture postcard, but a few cold rains along the Atlantic coastline had morphed Stony Point's townscape into dirty snow, mud and slop. Chilly, damp winds now blew, and foliage was not yet ready to awaken.

By the first Saturday in March, Alice and Annie stood in the second-floor hallway, both of them with their hands on their hips, surveying the near-empty rooms.

"I cannot believe how much stuff we've thrown or given away," Annie said.

"And I cannot believe what a huge write-off I'm going to get on my taxes this year with all my charitable donations!" Alice said.

"And I cannot believe I helped you haul everything off."

"What do you think best friends are for?"

"I can't argue with that," Annie said. "What I *really* cannot believe is how much space you seem to have now. This looks twice as big as it did before."

"I know. Just imagine how big the downstairs will look when we get done with that," Alice said.

Annie groaned loudly for effect. "Oh, my!" she exclaimed. "In the flush of victory for all we've done, I forgot all about the downstairs. I think I just block it out whenever I walk upstairs." The pair had moved some items into the dining room; they were using the room as temporary storage for the items Alice planned to keep. "What are you going to do about the furniture up here?"

"Wally told me not to worry about it. He and his helpers will move everything from room to room as they work on the walls and floors."

"Oh, that makes sense," Annie said. "I know you'll be glad when all of this work is finished," she added, poking her friend in the shoulder.

"That's probably true. I cannot believe how much lighter I feel already. Once we finish the downstairs, I'll actually be able to host parties here again. I'm looking forward to that, especially since it will actually be my very own home now. Plus, some of my clients have mentioned wanting to host a party, but they don't have the space in their homes. Everyone knows I give the best parties in town."

"And this purging and cleaning wasn't all bad," Annie said. "I've never seen Valerie and Grace down at the library look so excited to get donations. They'll be sorting through those books and magazines for *months*."

Alice laughed and then gave her best friend a big hug. "Now we get to do the fun part—pick out paint colors for the walls!"

*   *   *   *

At each Hook and Needle Club meeting, the colored-in blankets on the tracking poster inched a little higher, but it didn't seem like they would ever be able to fill in the very last one. Even the teen club felt discouraged—they'd only finished one blanket each, and seemed a little lost without Gwen, who was still trying to take it easy after her hospital stay.

Alice persisted in making the mystery recipes, but she now tested them at home rather than bringing them to the meetings. Most of them were as bad—or worse—than the first one she'd made.

By the first Hook and Needle Club meeting in March, they'd almost reached the halfway mark—fifty-two completed blankets. Seventeen outlines on the poster sported cheery colors, and some had been signed. As they prepared to leave the meeting, Alice asked Annie if she would mind going to the bank with her.

"I've got a few papers to sign, and I want to ask John what he might know about the Swanns," she said. "This mystery is truly driving me cuckoo. Why are so many of these recipes so terrible?"

"Sure, I'll go with you," Annie replied, wrapping her neck in a warm scarf. "I don't know why the recipes are so bad. You know, usually we get to the bottom of our mysteries a lot quicker than this. Of course, we've been slammed with the Haiti project, and then with Gwen being so sick and needing surgery. What I really hate is that you have spent so much money on ingredients, only for most of it to go to waste."

They headed down the slushy sidewalk toward the bank, being careful where they stepped. Alice's ankle had healed, but she didn't want to risk injuring it again.

"I'm more worried about my street cred than the money I'm spending," Alice said.

"Street cred?" Annie asked, just as they walked past The Cup & Saucer. "I didn't realize you had any. I'm not even sure what that is, for that matter."

"Yeah, my street cred. You know, that hip-hop term for credibility on the street," Alice explained. "Oh, do you care if we stop in at the diner? I want to talk to Jeff a minute, and I'd like to grab a Coke to take to John."

"Sure," Annie said, trailing her friend into The Cup & Saucer. She grabbed an empty chair near the front door and waited while Alice sailed to the back and cornered the owner.

"Hey Annie. Can I get you anything?" Peggy stood next to the table, her order pad at the ready.

"Not right now, Peggy. Thanks anyway. I'm just waiting while Alice talks to your boss."

Peggy rolled her eyes. "Alice has been bugging him to use some of the recipes—the ones that turned out OK, of course—in the restaurant. She's not giving up. But I'm not either, and I've told Jeff in no uncertain terms that he has to tell her no."

"Why's that? Besides the obvious?"

"Well, just because it turned out OK once doesn't mean it will again. Plus, she's just so insistent. And Marie's not a fan of trying new things. What she makes works just fine, and our customers are happy. And again, we still don't know where those recipes came from. They could belong to someone, and then we'd be stealing them by using them."

"Wow. I hadn't thought of that," Annie said.

Alice breezed up, a to-go cup in one hand. "Ready?"

"After you," Annie replied.

"See you later," Peggy called as they went back outside.

"What did you want to talk to Jeff about?" Annie casually asked as they once more made their way down the messy sidewalk. She'd thought about Peggy's opinion, and wondered what Alice had to say about it.

"Oh, I just want The Cup & Saucer to put a few of these recipes on the menu. But Jeff keeps saying no. And Marie won't even talk to me."

"At all? That doesn't sound like Marie." The Cup & Saucer's cook was usually quite kind and friendly.

"Oh, yeah, she'll talk to me," Alice said, waving her free hand around. "She just won't talk about the recipes. If I bring it up, she either changes the subject or flat out leaves the room. I just don't understand."

"Well, can you blame them, really? I mean, most of the recipes obviously aren't complete or something. Besides that, we don't know where they came from."

"They came from under my floor!" Alice exclaimed, continuing to wave her hand about.

When they arrived at the bank, Annie opened the door and followed her friend in. Allison, John's assistant, waved them over and offered them each a seat.

"John's on a phone call, but he said he'd be right out."

"Thanks, Allison!" Alice said.

A few minutes later, John came out and asked Allison to hold his calls. He then ushered Annie and Alice into his office and shut the door, gesturing for them to have a seat at his desk as he flipped open a file folder.

"I brought this for you," Alice said, handing him the cup.

He immediately unwrapped the straw, shoved it through the lid, and took a big swallow.

"Aaaah. Thanks, I needed that. Since Gwen's health scare, I'm pretty sure I've drunk more Coke than I previously had in my entire life. I'll have to wean myself off eventually."

"How is Gwen?" Annie piped up. "I haven't seen her in a few days."

"She's doing fine, thank the good Lord," John said. "I'm glad people are still visiting her. She's so used to being active, and Dr. Barnett told her to rest so her body can heal and her immune system can get stronger." He took another swig of the Coke. "All the visitors distract her and keep her from doing too much."

He opened the folder, pulled out a stack of papers, and handed Alice a blue pen.

"Anyway, thanks for stopping by, Alice. Here are the final loan papers for your signature. Of course, there will be more to sign when we do the actual closing, which we are trying to schedule for the 20th, but it's going to be a little tricky since the Swanns won't be able to come here to sign their portion. I'll be sending the paperwork to a partner bank for them to take care of that end."

Alice had known the Swanns, who lived in New York, probably wouldn't be able to make the trip. "Sounds complicated," she said.

"A little, but we'll get it worked out. Now, sign here ... and here ...."

Annie zoned out while John pointed out places to sign and answered Alice's questions. After handling the bookkeeping for the GM dealership back in Texas all those years, Annie had decided she wanted nothing more to do with financial information. At least, as little as she could help it.

"That's all we need for now. I'll let you know when I hear a final date for closing. But for now, congrats on almost owning your home!" John said after what seemed like hours, but had probably only been a few minutes.

"Thank you ever so much, John. You have no idea how appreciative I am of your help," Alice replied. "But I have another question. Has Gwen mentioned our mystery?"

"Yes, she has." He leaned his chair back and drained the last of the soda, throwing the cup in the trash can. "Something about some recipes you found in the carriage house?"

"Yes. Handwritten recipes, in a mason jar, hidden under a floorboard of what used to be the main bedroom, and that I now use as my guestroom. Mary Beth said she remembers that the Swanns only stayed in Stony Point during the summer, and that the food at their parties could be kind of—well, different."

John laughed. "Yes, the food they served could definitely be called different. I think it came from living in New York most of the year. They could be very adventurous when it came to food."

"You don't think they would have hidden the recipes, do you?" Annie asked.

"Probably not—and definitely not handwritten ones. Yvonne especially was very fastidious about her cookbooks. She even retyped the ones she collected and had them organized in a binder."

Alice sighed. "So I guess we're looking for someone who lived there when Captain Grey was alive."

"Not necessarily," he said, moving his chair forward and resting his elbows on the table. "Before they stopped coming down during the summer—right before you moved in, Alice—the Swanns occasionally rented out the carriage house during the winter. Best I can recall, the renters were families whose husbands either worked on boats or assisted with the renovation of Butler's Lighthouse. The women tended to work at the library or in one of the shops."

"I wonder if one of those families may have left the recipes?" Alice said.

"It's certainly possible," John said. "Why haven't you contacted the Swanns directly and asked them?"

"Well, I haven't wanted to mess something up in the negotiations by getting in touch with them," Alice replied. "After all, I've never really dealt with them directly, just their management company, and I've only met them the one time."

"I don't think you need to worry about that," John told her. He went to his desk, looked up the Swanns' number and jotted it on the back of one of his business cards, which he then handed to Alice. "I'm sure they won't mind hearing from you, especially now that we've worked everything out."

Allison knocked on the door and poked her head in. "John, I know you said to hold your calls, but Gwen says she needs to speak with you."

John shook hands with Alice and Annie. "Pardon me, ladies, for kicking you out, but the real boss calleth."

*   *   *   *

Malone's Hardware Store stayed open late on Thursday nights, and Ian and Annie had arranged to stop by after Town Hall closed to look through copies of *The Point*. They'd been meaning to do so for about a month, but had been unable to coordinate their schedules.

"Hey you two," Mike said, pulling on his left ear. Annie had noticed he did that when he was thinking. "Go on back and help yourself. My morgue is your morgue," he added with a laugh, using the newspaper term for the room containing previous editions, photos and notes on stories. "Thankfully, it's a lot neater and more organized than it used to be. Fiona and Greg spent a lot of time back there."

"We will have to thank your lovely wife and your reporter for doing all that the work," Ian said as he and Annie walked into the back room.

"This is definitely neater than the last time I tried to dig for clues in here," Annie said, looking around the crowded space. Copies of the newspaper had been stacked on shelves rather than flung about any which way, and the shelves had labels with dates neatly printed on them.

"It really is," Ian agreed. "Someday I'd like to have everything archived electronically so it can easily be used for research. Plus, these pages hold the history of Stony Point. I've done some preliminary research on getting that done, and it will be expensive. So, for now it will just have to be a long-term goal."

"That would be wonderful," Annie answered. "At least they've got the papers in date order now. That should help a bit. We know my grandparents bought Grey Gables and the carriage house in 1947, and that they renovated the carriage house in 1984. Gram sold it to the Swanns in 1990, and Alice started living there in 2008. We know we don't have to look at anything after that. Maybe focus on the summers when the Swanns would have been visiting."

Annie ambled along the shelves, running her fingers over the dates. She stopped when she got to some in the 1970s. "Oh! I didn't know Mike had been putting out the paper this long!"

"He hasn't," Ian told her. "His dad, Mike Sr., started the paper—and the hardware store for that matter—back in 1955, I think. Mike and I grew up together and spent many a happy hour in here playing with bolts and whatnot. At the time, Mike didn't have any interest in the paper, but he pretty much inherited both the store and the paper when his dad passed away. He grew to love being the town historian."

"Wow, I never thought about you two being friends

for so long," Annie said. "My unpredictable childhood prevented me from putting down permanent roots in any one place. Sometimes I'd spend the school year with my Aunt Susan in Texas if my folks were away on mission work. That, of course, is why I attended Texas A&M for college, and that's where I met Wayne. I spent time with my parents when they weren't on a missionary trip. When they were in the States, we did a lot of traveling around and visiting churches to raise money."

"And you spent your summers here with Betsy."

"Yes. Those were the best. I'm surprised you and I didn't meet each other then."

Ian chuckled. "Well, I am a few years older than you. I'm sure I didn't even notice you back then. After all, you would have been a mere kid, and I a suave teenager."

"Oh, yes, I keep forgetting about your advanced dotage," Annie teased him.

They pulled out stacks of papers from the early 1990s and started looking through them.

"So, did you ever want to go with your parents on their mission trips?" Ian asked. He replaced his first stack with another one, which he flipped through quickly.

"Sometimes, yes. I missed them terribly. But they wrote often and sent me tons of photos and presents on every major occasion that we were apart. I grew up knowing how much they loved me, and I felt pride in what they did to help the world at large." She finished looking through a pile of papers, put it back on the shelf, and grabbed a stack from the 1970s.

"I was also keenly aware that they wanted me to have as normal a childhood as I could. Of course, we knew a lot of missionaries and would attend conferences, and a lot of the missionary kids I knew seemed pretty miserable."

"How so?" Ian looked up from the papers. "By the way, I have no idea what we're looking for, but so far, no mention of the Swanns."

"I don't know either. Maybe the Hook and Needle Club can help raise funds to get the papers online. Seems we probably look at these more than anyone else."

"But first you have to finish Blanket Haiti."

"Yes, we do. Kate is convinced we'll never meet the goal."

"Definitely not with my help," Ian said. "I'm pretty hopeless at crocheting, despite your best efforts to teach me. But anyway, why do you say the missionary kids were miserable?"

"Well, all of them could be put into one of three categories. One: shy, withdrawn, and no social skills; two: bubbly, extroverted, and the life of the party; or three: the rebellious kid with lots of problems—drugs, trouble with the law, pregnancies, you name it. After spending a week at the conference with those kids every year, I knew my parents had chosen the right thing for me. I had social skills, friends, a family who loved and cared for me, and I didn't have to keep starting over all of the time. I think when missionary parents took their children with them, they would spend more time taking care of others than their own children, and it showed. My parents took care of me, just in a different way. For me it was a better way."

"That makes sense." Ian set aside a pile he'd gone through and started looking at another. "Oh, look—here's an article about one of the Swanns' parties. June 1993." Annie leaned over his shoulder and took in the photo of a crowd in front of the carriage house. "It reads: 'Residents Yvonne and Arthur Swann host a party to celebrate the first day of summer.'" He skimmed the article and then said, "Well, there doesn't appear to be anything useful here."

Mike came back into the morgue at seven o'clock. "All right, you sleuths. Sorry, but it's time for me to close up shop. Fiona doesn't like it when I get home late on lasagna night."

"Oh, no problem! I had no idea it had gotten so late," Annie said. She and Ian put away the last of the newspapers they'd pulled out.

"Did you find anything helpful?" Mike asked.

"Sadly, no. Well, only that your writing has improved over the years," Ian told him.

"Well, thank you—I think," he replied, turning out the lights in the morgue and then the main sales floor before locking up from the outside.

"See you two later," he said, striding down the street to his car.

"So now what?" Ian asked as they stood on the sidewalk. "Would you like to grab a bite to eat at Maplehurst Inn? We haven't been there in a while."

"Sure, I'd love to," Annie said.

They walked to the restaurant arm in arm.

～ 15 ～

At the next Hook and Needle Club meeting, Kate handed folded sheets of paper to the ladies gathered in the warm circle of chairs. Outside, it was dark and snowing. The bright colors of the shop made everyone feel cheerful, despite the terrible weather. Gwen was making her first Hook and Needle Club appearance since her operation.

After a few minutes of hugging and chatting, Kate handed a folded sheet of paper to each lady. "Here's more information on the orphanage, provided by our dear Reverend Wallace. He thought you'd want to read it so you'd know how important our efforts are." Kate said. She glanced at Gwen and Mary Beth, smiled, and then continued. "OK everyone, report in!"

Kate watched as Alice opened hers, glanced at the paper, and then shoved it in her bag. "Should I talk about the mystery now, or wait until later?" asked Alice.

"Wait until later. Tell us how you're doing on your blankets."

"I've got three to donate! One that I made, and two that I found as I cleaned up the carriage house." She got up and colored in an outline on the tracking poster in sunny yellow, and signed her name with a flourish in red.

"Great. Anyone else?" Kate tried to keep a straight face

206 D. Savannah George

as she watched the other ladies read the notes she'd handed out. The one she'd given to Alice only talked about the orphanage, while everyone else's had a different message.

Annie read hers, nodded, and then said, "I'm still working on several. I'm afraid I haven't finished any of them. And obviously Ian isn't here today. He said to give everyone his regards—and apologies for his inability to crochet well enough to help. He promises to purchase some blankets closer to the due date to make sure we meet our goal."

Kate knew Peggy would have a hard time not saying anything, so she skipped over her and went to Stella and Jason.

"I dug around and found three more blankets I made years ago, and here's a new one I just finished," Jason said. He, too, got up and made his mark on the poster. "I didn't realize how many I'd made over the years until I started looking. Since Mrs. Brickson is my only family, I never had anyone to give them to. I'm so glad they will finally be put to good use."

"Jason, be a dear and fill in another of those things," Stella said. "I've finished two more."

Gwen was next. "I didn't have a lot to keep me from going crazy with boredom," she said, "so I stayed busy on the orphanage blankets. I finished four and am almost through another. Jason, while you are at it, would you color in another and sign my name?"

Before anyone could continue, Gwen spoke up again. "Alice, I was wondering if you could come by Wedgewood after the meeting and help me with some hints for redecorating. It's almost spring, and I want to do some updates in my dining room. I'd like to put your Divine Décor expertise to work."

"Sure," Alice said. "I was going to lunch with Annie, but I'm sure that won't be a problem. Is that OK, Annie?"

Her friend smiled sweetly, glancing at her note from Kate. "Of course not," she said. "I'll see you back at your house later."

"My house!" Alice beamed. "That has a nice ring to it, doesn't it?"

Mary Beth added one more blanket to the box, and Peggy unfurled her second quilt. "I'm proud to say that Emily actually helped with this one: she picked out some of the fabric and sewed some of the stitches."

"Wonderful! That's fifteen blankets today, bringing us up to a grand total of sixty-seven," Kate said.

"I have to stop by Ocean View later this afternoon and pick up some more blankets from the residents," Annie said. "I don't know how many they've completed."

"Oh, good," Kate sighed. "We're over halfway there, and we still have almost three months to go. I've been so worried that the project was just too big to achieve."

"Nonsense," said Stella. "Ambitious, yes, but not un-attainable. I'm so proud of the way the community has pulled together. I keep forgetting to mention that visitors to the Cultural Center have really enjoyed our display of blankets and the story behind them. We put out a do-nation box and have collected about $500 so far for the church's mission trip."

"Oh! That's so exciting!" Kate exclaimed. "OK, Alice, now tell us your latest on the mystery."

"Well, unfortunately, I've not really got that much to tell. I think everyone has probably heard by now what Cecil Lewey said about not remembering anyone staying in the carriage house when the Holdens owned it."

Everyone in the room nodded.

"I signed some loan papers after the last meeting, and John told me it would be OK if I contacted the Swanns directly. I had been afraid to do so, in case it threw a wrench in the process of buying the carriage house. Apparently they occasionally rented it out during the winters. I've called several times, but they've acted very suspicious of my questions. They finally told me that they rarely used that bedroom during their summer visits, and they claim that they can't remember who rented the carriage house. Since the closing on the carriage house is so soon, I don't want to press harder and possibly jeopardize that. At this point, I'm completely stumped."

"Did you ever ask about having an expert look at the handwriting?" Stella asked.

"I did, and John told me that it would probably be more complicated and costly than I'd be willing to pay. He gave me his expert's phone number, who told me the same thing. Apparently, to get a full report, we'd have to hire a chemist to do ink-dating to see how old the paper and ink is; a linguist would be needed to analyze the language used; and then the handwriting guy could determine if it appeared to be naturally written or copied."

"My goodness," said Peggy. "That does sound complicated."

"It is! The handwriting expert also told me that he

wouldn't be able to tell the age or gender of the writer. So, needless to say, I decided not to pursue that angle, even though it would be interesting."

"Ian and I looked through back issues of *The Point*, but didn't find anything either," Annie said. She felt the tips of her ears start to turn red, but was determined to ignore it. "But in the good news category, some other papers ran stories on our project, so maybe we'll get even more blankets."

*   *   *   *

Fifteen minutes after the meeting had ended, all the Hook and Needle Club members but Alice and Gwen reassembled at A Stitch in Time. The note that Kate had given to everyone but Alice had read: "Alice closes on the carriage house soon. Let's throw her a surprise party. Meet back here fifteen minutes after the meeting. Shhh!"

"Whew! Thank you all for not spilling the beans!" Kate said after everyone was seated again. "Peggy, I especially worried about you saying something."

Peggy laughed. "I worried about that too. Didn't you notice I spent most of the meeting with my head down? I thought my face alone might give it away!"

"I'm so glad Gwen asked Alice to go to her house. It was a great way to make sure she doesn't come back here," Kate said. "OK, as we all know, Alice is closing on the carriage house sometime this month—right, Annie?"

"Right. It depends on when they can coordinate with the Swanns' bank. But when we talked to John, he hoped for the 20th of March."

"So I'm thinking we throw her a housewarming party on the last day of March, which just happens to fall on a Saturday. What do you guys think?" Kate asked.

They all agreed it was an excellent idea. Kate volunteered Vanessa and Mackenzie to design invitations for the party. "I don't know if they'll get school credit for it, but I'm sure they'd love to do it."

"There is one problem," Annie interjected. "We really can't hold it at the carriage house—the downstairs is a disaster, what with moving everything out of the way so that Wally can get started renovating the upstairs. It would be weird to hold a housewarming party that's not at her house, but I think she'd be really embarrassed to have everyone see it right now."

"What about having it at Maplehurst Inn?" Mary Beth asked. "Linda Hunter loves Alice. The inn has that library that's perfect for parties, and I'm sure Linda would be happy to have her staff cater. It should also be easy to get Alice there without letting her in on the secret. Annie, you could invite her to dinner to celebrate the closing, and we'd all be there, waiting."

"Maplehurst Inn would be perfect," Stella said.

"Oooh, that would be a great surprise!" Peggy exclaimed. "I'll handle the food arrangements with Maplehurst; Jeff might be willing to supply some food as well."

"Another problem," Kate said. "We're too busy making blankets to create gifts for her."

"That's true," Peggy said. "I couldn't possibly find the time to make anything else, and a store-bought gift would be a serious faux pas, especially from us."

"Well, trust me, as someone who just helped her get rid of a lot of stuff, Alice does not need anything else," Annie said. "I have an idea. Remember when Alice mentioned that I had found the plans from when my grandparents had renovated the carriage house? Well, what do you all think about pitching in and having one of them framed? Some of them look really neat."

"I like that idea," said Stella. "But didn't you already give them to her? Wouldn't she notice if they were missing?"

Annie laughed. "Trust me, no. Not in the bedlam that is a major remodeling project. I guarantee you that I can spirit those plans away, and she'll never notice."

"Wally mentioned he couldn't believe the difference in the upstairs. When he came home after his first consult, he said he figured she'd never get it ready to start," Peggy said.

"She didn't. *We* did," Annie said with a laugh.

"Well, sounds like we've got a plan," Kate said. "Let me know what you all find out!"

* * * *

Kate had that Saturday off from work. She'd hoped that, in order to spend time with her daughter, Vanessa and Mackenzie would stay in and work on the invite for Alice's housewarming party, but Vanessa had left before ten o'clock.

"Bye, Mom!" she'd hollered on her way out the door. "I'm gonna hang out with Hannah and Holly and Mackenzie. We're going to work on our blankets. See you later."

This learning-to-let-go part of parenting totally sucks, Kate thought to herself as soon as the door slammed.

It really sucks. She walked to the window, pulled aside the curtain and watched as her daughter carefully backed out of the driveway.

For someone who'd had no interest in cars or driving just a month or so ago, Vanessa had turned into a very good and careful driver. She even washed her car every week, especially after Kate noted that the salt left on the road after a Maine winter would quickly set up corrosion on the automobile. Kate had to give Harry credit. He'd come through, and in a big way. He'd even given her money to cover the car insurance.

Kate sighed and let the curtain fall back. Mary Beth had made her promise to start putting together a crochet pattern book, so she planned to spend the day looking through her notes and the magazine articles she'd had published, and picking out her favorite patterns. She sighed again and began to work.

*   *   *   *

Kate jumped when she heard the door into the kitchen slam. She looked at her watch—two o'clock. She'd been so engrossed in looking through all her patterns, she'd completely lost track of time. And she had forgotten to eat lunch. Her stomach grumbled, reminding her of the oversight.

"Mom! I'm home!" Vanessa called out, walking into the living room. "Holy cow! It looks like the copier room at school exploded."

"I know!" Kate said, rubbing her eyes and pulling

back her hair. "I had no idea I had created so many different patterns."

"Where were they all hiding?" Vanessa asked as she tiptoed around the stacks and sank into the chair. "I didn't even know our house could hold this much! And why do you have them all out? What are you doing?"

"Well, Mary Beth has been after me to put together a book of my patterns and try to get it published. She made me promise to work on it today."

"Cool!" Vanessa bounced on her hands. "My mom, the famous pattern-maker."

"As to where they all were hiding—well, in practically every corner of the house. Up in the attic, under my bed, on the bookshelf, in the garage. I actually think I may have enough for a series of books. You know, afghans and sweaters and socks and scarves and hats, from beginner to expert."

"What about those animals you crocheted me when I was little?"

"Oh heavens. I forgot all about those, and I'm not sure where those patterns even are."

"I bet I know," Vanessa said, getting up and doing the tiptoe walk around and to her bedroom. A few minutes later she reappeared, digging through a small box. She pulled out some papers from the bottom. "They're right here, with all my baby things."

"I knew I kept you around for something!" Kate laughed. "How'd your blanket-making go?"

"Good. Holly and Hannah are working on finishing up the borders of theirs. They look really cute. And Mackenzie has started a new one."

"Hooray!" Kate said. "Now be a dear and help your poor old mom clean up this mess."

*   *   *   *

The last day of March, and the day of Alice's surprise party, finally arrived. As John had thought, and to Kate's vast relief, Alice had closed on the carriage house on March 20th, making her the official owner.

Kate had inadvertently become the party coordinator, but even she had to admit everything looked perfect. The ladies had hung streamers in Maplehurst Inn's library, and Vanessa and Mackenzie and a few of their friends had made a banner. It hung over the fireplace and read "Congrats to Alice, the New Home Owner!" in bold colors, decorated with abstract flowers and butterflies. An easel sat near the fireplace, covered by a gold damask cloth.

A small table with a matching tablecloth was placed near the entrance.

The girls had also made a big card for everyone to sign. Kate had brought the markers for the tracking poster with her, and the guests—male and female—seemed to be having fun writing in the card. The attendees seemed to be a cross section of Alice's friends and clients, along with all of the Hook and Needle Club members, of course.

Peggy had apparently found her true calling: catering events. Linda told Kate that she'd never seen anything like it.

"If Jeff wouldn't kill me, I would hire Peggy to be my catering director," Linda had said. "Heck, I still might.

There's no reason we couldn't work with The Cup & Saucer on events."

The beautifully decorated table was covered with trays of finger foods and sweets, along with confetti, streamers and small bouquets of flowers from the local florist. Linda and her staff stood by to hand out drinks and make sure the trays stayed filled.

Gwen sat in a paisley-covered wingback chair and was still the center of attention; everyone who walked in the room gave her a hug.

"I'm so glad you could make it," Kate told Gwen.

"Wouldn't miss it!" Gwen said. "I'm glad I'm able to make our meetings now, but the Teen Hook and Needle Club meetings on the same day was just a bit more than I've been ready for yet. How are they doing without me?"

"Oh, they talk about you constantly," Kate told her. "It's 'Mrs. Palmer this' and 'Mrs. Palmer that' and 'Mrs. Palmer said *this* is how you do this stitch.' They'll be really excited to see you. Most of them should be here any minute."

Gwen looked at her watch. "What time is Annie supposed to arrive with Alice? It's already six forty-five."

"At seven. Hopefully everyone else will get here before they do. But knowing Alice, she and Annie will probably be late."

"Do you think she suspects anything?"

"I hope not," Kate laughed. "If she does, she hasn't let on."

More people trickled in, including Vanessa and her friends; Kate left Gwen to go welcome them. Ally, one of the inn's waitresses, circulated the room, taking empty glasses back to the kitchen.

At five minutes until seven, Kate tapped a spoon against a glass, and the room quieted down. "OK, everybody, quiet voices please. Annie and Alice should be here any second. Rachel, the front desk clerk, is going to call my cellphone when they walk in. Everyone, make sure you have a glass in hand so we can toast Alice when she arrives."

She'd barely stopped talking when her phone rang. "OK everyone, they're here! Places!"

The assemblage immediately stopped talking, shuffled around so they faced the doors that Kate had hastily closed, and raised their glasses.

They could hear Alice's voice echo around the lobby. "Annie, I don't see why you insisted I dress up for dinner. You know they don't have a dress code here."

"Yeah, yeah, yeah. They let everyone in," they heard Annie reply. "I just wanted us to have a nice dinner. All we've eaten lately is soup."

"Why aren't we going to the dining room? Why are we going to the library? Why are you dragging me through all creation?"

They heard a fumbling at the doors, Annie saying, "Hush," and then the doors swung open.

Everyone yelled "Surprise!"

Alice's face went pale. Kate handed her a glass of champagne, which she downed in one gulp.

"What am I being surprised for? I'm not dying, am I?" she asked, to a chorus of laughter.

"No, dear Alice, we are throwing you a housewarming party!" Annie said, escorting her into the room.

"Hear, hear!" several in the room called out as Annie led Alice to the fireplace and the covered easel.

"And since we *all* know you do not need a single thing, and since none of us had time to make you something special, we got you this!"

With a flourish, Annie removed the gold damask to reveal the framed blueprint of the carriage house. Alice burst into tears.

*   *   *   *

"I still can't believe you guys did this," Alice said a few hours later. "And that I burst into tears. How embarrassing."

Most of the guests—and the food—were gone, but the core Hook and Needle Club members and some of the teens still remained.

"So you had no idea we had this in the works?" Kate asked.

"Nope, not a clue." Alice nibbled on a petit four. "I never in a million years would have guessed that you'd throw me a housewarming party, especially since I've lived there for so long already."

"But now it's yours," Kate said. "We decided it would make for a perfect celebration. Besides, it's not like you had a party when you moved in."

"No. No, I did not. I wouldn't have wanted one either." She took a few bites of a watercress sandwich, and after swallowing, said, "Seriously. How did you guys pull this off?"

"Remember that day I got you to come with me to talk about some redecorating after a meeting?" Gwen asked.

"Yeah?"

"And I'd handed out information about the orphanage?" Kate added.

"I guess. So?"

"Well, yours had info about the orphanage. Everyone else's told them to come back in fifteen minutes so we could start planning this party."

"For once in my life, I am practically speechless. And I love that you had one of the blueprints framed."

"That was Annie's idea," Kate told her. "She said she could get it from your house and you'd never know."

"Well, she sure did," Alice admitted. "You guys are the best!"

~ 16 ~

*T*he weeks passed quickly for the members of the Hook and Needle Club. They continued to collect and make blankets, and the tracking poster slowly filled up. The weather began to improve until spring temperatures arrived around Memorial Day, and the foliage began to bloom.

The smells of spring are salve for a soul weary of winter, Annie thought as she ambled through her garden, and then she wondered when was the last time that she had waxed so poetic. But it was true. The smells of honeysuckle, roses, lilacs, hyacinths, and Easter lilies all made her smile and made her heart feel lighter. And she wasn't the only one; everyone's spirits seemed elevated with the arrival of spring.

By the first Hook and Needle Club meeting in June, they only lacked ten blankets to meet their goal. Ian had stopped attending the meetings, deciding it was pointless for him to continue. Stella had sent Jason on a few errands, so just regulars were in attendance.

"Kate, you look beside yourself with happiness," Annie told her as they all admired the poster. "Look at what we've accomplished!"

"Oh, I am. Very much so. I had my doubts along the way, but we're so close, there's no way we won't meet the goal."

"I agree," chimed in Mary Beth. "And I have exciting

news to share, which no doubt Kate won't tell you because she's too modest to tell anyone."

Annie noticed that Kate started blushing. Mary Beth ignored her and continued. "Our very own Kate Stevens has put together *ten* books of her crochet patterns, and we're shopping them around to see who might be interested in publishing them."

The ladies in the circle started clapping, making Kate blush even more.

"It's about time, Kate," Annie said. "Share that gift of yours with a larger audience."

After the congratulations died down, Alice spoke up. "I am so frustrated with our lack of progress in solving this mystery. It has never taken us this long. Anyway, I brought everything Annie and I found with me. I haven't paid much attention to anything but the recipes, which clearly have been no help."

"But that didn't stop you from making us try them," Peggy said.

Alice ignored her and continued. "It occurred to me that the other items might spark an idea."

She pulled everything out of her bag and spread it on the table: the square of brown fabric, the spatula, the bottle of spices, the knife, the mason jar, and the recipes, which she'd placed in folders and kept organized after she and Annie had gone through them.

"Hmmm ... I wonder if that knife was used in a murder," Peggy said.

"Murder? Gosh, I hope not!" Alice said.

"I wonder if I should ask Chief Edwards to look into

that," Annie said. "Maybe it could help him with an unsolved crime."

"I, for one, doubt that knife was used to murder anyone," Stella said, her knitting needles clacking furiously. "Not that it couldn't be used to hurt someone, but it would require a lot of work to do so. The blade is too short. Anyway, it looks like a tourné knife to me."

"What's that?" Peggy asked, picking it up to peer at it.

"A specialized paring knife. They're used to cut decorative garnishes, like for radishes and mushrooms. My cook back in New York had one. They're not usually found in a typical kitchen."

"What about this old spatula?" Mary Beth asked, waving it around. "Alice, did you use this when making the recipes? Maybe it's what caused the disgusting tastes."

"No, as a matter of fact, I did not," Alice retorted.

The ladies picked up the items and started passing them around the circle. When the bottle got to Stella, she suddenly went very still.

"I know this name and this label!" she exclaimed, touching the ornate label carefully. "The Spice Café used to be a well-known and very elegant restaurant in New York. My father took me there to celebrate my sixteenth and seventeenth birthdays." Stella paused, a faraway look in her eye. "Going there made me feel very grown up. Unfortunately, by my eighteenth birthday, the place had closed. I remember feeling so very disappointed."

"It never even occurred to me that these could have been recipes from a restaurant," Alice said. "And I never thought about the label. We had such a problem just opening the jar with the recipes inside that I never tried to open the bottle."

"And I don't believe you ever mentioned the name," Stella said. "I definitely would have recognized it. The restaurant called itself The Spice Café because their claim to fame was a special, expensive spice in most of their recipes."

"Which spice?" Peggy asked.

"I have no idea," Stella said. "They kept it a closely guarded secret."

*   *   *   *

That afternoon, Annie and Alice used Annie's laptop to research the restaurant. Annie sat at Gram's desk, and Alice had pulled up a chair to sit next to her.

After a few clicks, Annie turned the screen to show Alice. "OK, a search for 'The Spice Café' isn't helping. There are over ninety-three thousand results."

"Well, try 'The Spice Café in New York City.'"

"All right." Annie typed it in, and then clicked through a number of links. "No good. Fewer results, but none of them appear to be what we're looking for."

Alice sighed. "OK, so it went out of business in the year between Stella's seventeenth and eighteenth birthdays. How old do you think she is?"

"Well, I know she and Gram used to be close, so they have to be about the same age. Gram was born in 1922. I think Stella is a couple of years younger; maybe she was born in 1923 or 1924."

"OK, so look for The Spice Café in New York in—uh—1938."

"Bingo," Annie said after a few taps. She pulled up some newspaper articles about the restaurant. "Stella wasn't kidding! It looks like The Spice Café really was a famous restaurant. Look at these reviews!"

They scrolled through review after review, all of them glowing.

"Amazing tastes ... don't know how they do it ... won't share their secrets ... have to reserve your table at least a month in advance," Alice read.

"Oh, look, here's an article from 1935 about the restaurant," Annie said. She read part of the article aloud. "'Earl Snyder and Francis Bowman have opened a new concept in eating. The Spice Café serves traditional French dishes like bouillabaisse and rouille, along with seafood dishes like cod and striped bass. Their dessert menu includes homemade favorites like fudge, along with more traditional items like rice pudding, custards, and cheesecake. Mr. Snyder tells this reporter that the name of the restaurant comes from a secret spice they include in many of their recipes.'"

"I wonder if the fudge I made was similar to their fudge!" Alice exclaimed.

"Could be," Annie replied, scrolling through more articles. "Uh, oh. Here's one from January 1942. 'This reviewer is disappointed to say that The Spice Café, long one of my favorite restaurants in our fair city, is no longer serving the best food in town. On a recent evening, hardly anyone frequented the café, and their normally excellent braised chicken with risotto can only be described as a fiasco.' And here's one from later in the same year: 'Francis Bowman has permanently closed The Spice Café, once one of New York's finest and most famous restaurants.' That's sad."

"Sad, yes, but what happened to the other owner, Earl? Why would such a famous restaurant go under?" Alice asked.

"I would guess it closed because the food quality went downhill," Annie replied. "I mean, look at all these terrible reviews. Maybe that bottle of spice had something to do with it."

"Or maybe Mr. Snyder did the cooking, and after he left, Mr. Bowman hired lousy chefs."

"But why would a co-owner just leave?"

"Could be anything. Happens all the time in the food industry," Alice said. "See if you can find anything on Mr. Bowman."

After some more typing and clicking around, Annie announced, "Here's his obituary. It says that Francis Bowman died in 1956 with no heirs or family. That's also very sad."

"Is there no mention of The Spice Café?"

"Nope. It just says that he had owned various restaurants."

Alice leaned back in her chair. "OK," she said. "So Francis Bowman is a dead end. Literally. So what about Earl Snyder?"

After a few more minutes of Annie clicking around and reading articles, she had the answer. "Earl and his wife Camilla opened another restaurant in New York, called Earl's Diner. Looks like it wasn't quite as successful as their other venture. According to their obituaries, their son Harold and his family inherited the restaurant, and they have a daughter, Kathryn Snyder, who lives—" Annie stopped in mid-sentence, stunned.

"Where?" Alice demanded.

"Right here in Stony Point!"

*   *   *   *

"A Kathryn Snyder is a resident at Seaside Hills Assisted Living, and she's ninety-one, which puts her around the right age, but it's possible she's not the Kathryn we're looking for," Annie said after she hung up the phone. "You remember Katrina, the activities director? Well, she said Kathryn's napping right now, but that we could stop by in an hour or so. I wonder if this Kathryn is the same person that Mary Beth and Kate said had stopped by A Stitch in Time. They couldn't remember her name, but I'm pretty sure it started with a K."

Alice sunk back into Annie's floral couch with a sigh. "Maybe it is! However, I don't know if I can wait that long. And I sure hope this is the right Kathryn. This mystery is driving me crazy! Not to mention, I'm not exactly thrilled that my baking mojo has been so off lately. Maybe Kathryn can explain why."

"You're telling me. I want the old Alice back! The one who bakes things that taste divine, not the one who makes the repulsive stuff you've been foisting on us lately."

Annie ducked as her friend chucked a decorative pillow at her.

*   *   *   *

An hour later, the two friends arrived at Seaside Hills Assisted Living in Annie's trusted Malibu. They would have taken Alice's perky red Mustang, but Alice had just washed it, and she felt certain it would rain the second she drove it anywhere.

Alice had wrapped all of the items in the brown cloth and stashed it in her bag, which she retrieved from the backseat as soon as Annie parked.

When they entered the common room, a short, slender elderly woman stood up to greet them. She wore a plain, green linen dress with a white sweater over her shoulders.

"Are you Kathryn Snyder?" Alice asked.

"Yes, dear, I am," she said, reaching out a hand for them both to shake. "But you can call me Kitty. My mother's the only one who ever called me Kathryn, and then only when I had done something bad."

"It's so very nice to meet you. I'm Annie Dawson, and this is my friend, Alice MacFarlane."

Kitty led them to a small table near the window, which gave them a good view of the garden and all the beautiful flowers.

"So, how may I help you?" she asked after they'd been seated. "Katrina only said you had some questions for me."

"Yes, we do," said Alice. "Have you bought crafting supplies from A Stitch in Time?"

Kitty looked surprised. "Why yes, I have. I've knitted a few blankets for the Haiti project. The owner is just the sweetest thing." She paused, and then added, "But that's not why you're here, is it?"

"Not really," Alice said, "but I'm not quite sure where to

start." She pulled the cloth-wrapped package from her bag, opened it, and began to spread everything on the table.

Kitty's eyes got bigger and bigger as each new item emerged and was placed on the square of faded brown fabric: the spatula and bottle of spices, the dull knife and the mason jar, and then the file folders with the recipes.

"Do you recognize any of this?" Alice asked.

"Indeed I do," Kitty said as she covered her eyes with her hands and started to cry.

Annie got up and retrieved a box of tissues from a nearby table, handing them to the distressed woman.

"Thank you," Kitty said, uncovering her face and taking one. "You must have found these in Captain Grey's carriage house."

"Yes, we did. I live in the carriage house now, and Annie owns Grey Gables," said Alice. "Did you live there? Was it you who hid these things beneath the floorboard of the bedroom?"

"How much do you know about these things?" Kitty asked, wiping her eyes and clenching the tissue in her left hand.

"We know that they came from The Spice Café in New York City, which was owned by Earl Snyder and Francis Bowman, and closed in 1942. Are you Earl's daughter?" Annie asked gently. "What happened to the restaurant? And how did you end up here?"

Kitty sighed and straightened her shoulders.

"Yes, I'm Earl Snyder's daughter. You want to know how I came to be here in Stony Point? Well, it's kind of a long story, and it's one I'm not terribly proud of."

Alice reached out and held Kitty's right hand. "We have plenty of time, and we'd love to hear your story, if you don't mind telling us."

Kitty smiled wistfully and wiped her eyes again. "When I was younger, my parents owned a small restaurant. Papa had been in the war, and he fell in love with saffron when he was stationed in Italy and worked as an Army cook. He brought some back with him—oh, I guess it would have been in 1918 or so. Before I was born, anyway."

"I don't know if I've ever bought saffron or used it in a recipe," Alice said.

"Most likely not, dear. Saffron is the world's most expensive spice. Just a tiny bit costs an astonishing amount of money. It can take up to 250,000 purple saffron crocus flowers to make just one pound of the spice." She took another tissue and wiped her eyes again.

"But Papa brought some back with him and experimented until he came up with his very own secret spice recipe. Of course, the main ingredient is saffron, but he included other spices as well. After that, Papa experimented some more and figured out how to use his spice in various dishes, things you wouldn't expect."

"Like bread pudding?" Alice asked, suddenly realizing why her attempts had fallen short.

"Yes, indeed, like bread pudding," Kitty smiled. "Francis Bowman was a regular customer at my parents' restaurant, and he convinced Papa to partner with him. Mr. Bowman seemed like a good businessman, and he had all kinds of ideas about how to make the restaurant bigger. In 1935, when I was thirteen, they opened The Spice Café. Papa ran the kitchen, and Mr. Bowman took care of the books. He was very smart, and his ideas helped the restaurant greatly. The Depression didn't seem to affect us at all." As she talked, Kitty's hands caressed the items one by one. She picked up the spice bottle and said, "We only made up one bottle at a time to prevent anyone from duplicating it. This is the only one left in the world."

She stared at it, holding the bottle tightly in both hands. Her voice became faint.

"I practically grew up there—if I wasn't in the kitchen, I cleaned tables or washed linens, like this napkin, or arranged flowers for the centerpieces."

Annie and Alice exchanged glances, and Alice mouthed, "Napkin!" Annie imagined that Alice was mentally smacking herself in the forehead. Neither one of them had even thought that the piece of cloth might be a napkin.

"The café became a huge success, bigger than Papa had ever dreamed. Famous people like Charlie Chaplin and Dorothy Day would dine with us. Restaurant critics had nothing but good things to say. Couples got engaged in our dining room, and then they'd come back every year to celebrate their wedding anniversary. Everyone speculated about our secret ingredient, but we never told. No one told. We even concealed it as much as possible from the employees. Those who had to know about the spice also had to sign an agreement saying they would never reveal it."

Kitty's face had transformed, gotten lighter, and Alice and Annie could both see the beautiful young woman she once had been.

"Our family prospered. Papa was so proud he could

finally buy us—Mother, my older brother, Harold, and me—the finest things. We moved into a beautiful brownstone, and I had my own room and books and lovely dresses. We were all so happy."

She set the bottle down and shook her head as if clearing away years of memories.

"Then, in 1941, after six years of great success with the café, Mr. Bowman bilked my father out of all the restaurant's earnings, stopped paying suppliers, and ruined our family fortune. Somehow he managed to run Papa off, so he had no money and no job. We had to move from our nice brownstone to a tenement."

She choked up and took another tissue from the box.

"And worst of all, Papa's heart had broken. He loved that restaurant. He loved the people who came in to eat, and he loved how happy the food made them. He was so proud that he had been able to give us such a nice life, and he was grief-stricken that it had all been stolen from us. He wouldn't cook anymore, not even for his family."

Kitty took another tissue and wiped her eyes again. Alice and Annie sat spellbound.

"Papa didn't do anything to Mr. Bowman, and I wanted him to get even. But Papa wouldn't. He'd just shake his head and say we'd be OK. Meanwhile, Mr. Bowman still ran the restaurant, using Papa's secret spice and all his recipes. I decided that since no one else would do it, I would ruin him like he ruined us. So one night, I broke into the restaurant and stole all of this."

Kitty reached for the pile of recipes.

"These pages are more than mere recipes," she said,

handling the papers gently as she looked through them. "I was angry, so I stole the very recipe that made the food so wonderful and the restaurant famous—the special spice mixture. Without it, The Spice Café couldn't make the dishes they were known for. And I stole many of those recipes too, so Mr. Bowman wouldn't be able to even try."

Kitty explained that stealing the bottle and the spice recipe meant no one would be able to make any of the dishes ever again.

"This is the spice recipe," she said, holding up one of the smaller sheets.

"We never could figure that one out!" said Alice. "It looks like hieroglyphics!"

Kitty smiled. "Papa did that on purpose. Only a very few of us knew what these symbols meant. And we didn't even include it in the other recipes—we wrote that particular ingredient and the amount needed in code."

"Well, I for one am *very* relieved," Alice said, laughing. "I tried making a lot of those, and they mostly turned out awful. I thought I'd lost my baking mojo!"

"I was starting to think that too," Annie said. "I was afraid I'd have to pick up the baking torch from you, and it would have melted straightaway in my incapable hands!"

Kitty laughed with them. "You tried to make the recipes? Of course they tasted awful—they lacked the secret spice."

"So what happened after you took everything?" Alice asked.

"I didn't know what to do, so I fled the city by bus. We stopped for a break here in Stony Point, and I decided that

I'd gone far enough. No one would find me here, and besides, I was tired of riding and tired of my fellow passengers!"

Kitty explained that she had asked around and learned that Captain Grey was looking for a housekeeper, so she applied and he hired her on the spot.

"He was a sweet old man, not very demanding, and he let me live in the top of the carriage house. I promptly ripped up a floorboard in my bedroom and hid everything underneath it. You probably noticed the board was different."

Alice and Annie nodded.

"I never could get the original piece to fit again, so I went to the sawmill and got a board to replace the plank, covered it with a rug, and tried to forget about it. I kept Grey Gables spotless and made Captain Grey the best meals I could. It was my own form of penance, I think. When he got too feeble, he sold the entire place to the Holdens—I think it was in 1946 or '47.

"They were very kind, but clearly did not have money to keep me on. I quickly found other work as a housekeeper, which I did until I retired. I never moved back to New York, though I was quite often homesick for the big city and the restaurants and the shopping, and of course, my family. But I was too ashamed of what I had done to tell my parents, and I knew if I saw them I wouldn't be able to keep the secret any longer. We just stayed in touch by post, and later by telephone."

Annie put her hand on the older woman's arm. "I'm sorry—this must be difficult to talk about."

"Actually, I'm kind of relieved," Kitty said. "It's been a burden, keeping this secret for so long."

"Is your brother still alive?" Annie asked. "Have you seen him?"

"Oh yes. Papa gave Earl's Diner to Harold, and Harold gave it to his kids. My brother still works a little every day. And we try to visit each other at least once a year."

"Well, now you have something amazing to give him and his children," Annie said.

"My nieces and nephews, they're all grown up now. But yes. I will give them these recipes and teach them how to make the spice. I've never forgotten, you know."

"In that case, I happily return these to their rightful owner," Alice said. "I will no longer try to make these recipes. I've decided I much prefer selling Princessa jewelry and Divine Décor—and baking what I know will come out right."

*   *   *   *

The Hook and Needle Club meeting was just getting under way the next week when Annie, Alice, and Kitty walked in. Everyone looked up when they came through the door.

"Guess what, everyone?" Alice announced grandly. "We've solved our mystery. And here she is! Miss Kitty Snyder."

— Epilogue —

Every parking space in downtown Stony Point had a car in it, and vehicles were parked up the side streets. A van for a Portland television station sat outside the Cultural Center, its giant microwave antenna reaching up into the blue sky of a beautiful June day.

Inside, the Cultural Center buzzed with activity—a large, well-dressed crowd was celebrating the culmination of Blanket Haiti. Tables that Alice had beautifully decorated boasted food catered by The Cup & Saucer and Maplehurst Inn. Peggy and Linda strolled around, making sure the platters stayed full and that the guests had everything they needed.

A guy holding a TV camera and a reporter dressed in a light summer suit stood in front of colorful blankets spilling out of boxes. A group of ladies clustered nearby, waiting nervously.

Annie and Alice stood at the back of the room, munching on cucumber sandwiches and drinking punch. "This is so delightful, and your decorations look amazing," Annie said.

"They do, don't they? I had a lot of fun doing it," Alice replied.

The friends looked around at all the familiar faces—the other members of the Hook and Needle Club;

Vanessa, Mackenzie, and the girls in the teen group; Cecil Lewey, Steph, Janelle, and other crafters from Ocean View Assisted Living; and the Seaside Hills contingent of Joan, Frieda, Viola, Estelle, and Katrina. Even Harry Stevens was in attendance, but Annie thought he looked a mite uncomfortable in his khakis and sport coat.

Her heart fluttered when she saw Ian walk in.

"Annie, are you sure you don't want to be on TV?" he asked when he reached them. "After all, you're the one who got them here." He put his arm around her shoulders, and for once, she didn't feel her ears start to light up.

"No thank you," she laughed. "Besides, this is really *Kate's* project, and Peggy really wanted the spotlight. I for one wasn't going to stand in her way."

"Oh look, Alice, there's Kitty!" Annie exclaimed when she saw the slender woman enter.

"I'm so glad!" Alice said, taking a sip of her punch. "She told me she would try to make it, and that she hoped her family would join her." Alice glanced at Kitty and then added, "It looks like they did, or else those people are just following her for no reason."

Ian chuckled. "Kitty's the person who hid the items in the carriage house, right?"

"Right," Annie replied.

Moments later, Kitty had made it through the crowd. "Alice, Annie, I'd like you to meet my family. This is my brother, Harold, and his children, Heather and Dane." She paused as they all shook hands, and Annie introduced Ian.

"How delightful to meet you all," Harold rumbled. "So, you're the ladies who found my father's recipes?"

"Yes, we are," Alice said. "I own the carriage house, where Kitty lived when she first moved to Stony Point. Kitty told me you three still own Earl's Diner. Are you using the recipes in the restaurant?" Alice asked.

"Oh yes," Heather said. "Dad always told us stories, but I never really believed him until Kitty gave us everything and taught us how to make the spice mixture."

"And I inherited Grandpa's love of experimentation, so I'm having a ball trying to create recipes of my own," Dane interjected.

Annie couldn't help but smile at the family and how happy they looked.

"All right, everyone," the guy with the TV camera called out. "Please quiet down." He checked his headset. "OK, we're live in ... three, two, one."

As he pointed, the reporter lifted her microphone and smiled broadly.

"I'm Christina Archer, reporting live from the Cultural Center in Stony Point." The pretty brunette paused and gestured to the crowd behind her. "I'm here because of an extraordinary group of women and men who came together to make the blankets you see behind me for an orphanage in Haiti. With me is Kate Stevens, who spearheaded this effort, which they dubbed 'Blanket Haiti.'" She turned to Kate, who stood on her right. "Good evening, Kate. Please tell me how this came about."

"Thank you so much for coming to Stony Point, Christina. Members of our community church are leaving on a mission trip to Haiti in a week, where they will work with an orphanage and help build a school. After reading an article in January in our local paper, *The Point*, I felt like we just had to do something to help."

"And what was that?"

"To make blankets for the children of the orphanage. The members of our local crafting group, the Hook and Needle Club, wholeheartedly agreed, and then the entire community pitched in. Peggy Carson here is one of our members."

"Hello, Peggy," Christina said as Peggy walked to her left side. "What did you do for the project?"

"I made quilts, including this one," Peggy said, holding up a green-and-white creation. "My daughter, Emily, also helped me."

"Wonderful. I understand that some high school students pitched in as well."

"Yes, they did. Let me introduce Vanessa Stevens and Mackenzie Martel," Peggy told her.

"Hello," Christina said, as Peggy moved back and the teens took her place. "So tell us what your contribution was."

"We started a Teen Hook and Needle Club," Mackenzie said. "The ten girls waving back there are our club members."

Vanessa added, "We contributed a total of thirty knitted and crocheted blankets that we made ourselves." Behind